SHIP
OF
THESEUS

by Sandra Wagner

Ship of Theseus
by Sandra Wagner

Editor: Gail Sullivan
Art Direction: Rebekkah Dreskin

Published by Rocket Science Productions

ISBN-13: 978-1-945355-37-0
eISBN: 978-1-945355-38-7
Library of Congress Control Number: 2016956005

This is dedicated to my partner, June, who simply asked "What are you waiting for?" And to, Doris, my mentor, and teacher.

PROLOGUE

March 2150

Tim woke to the sound of the alarm at four-thirty. He rolled over and turned the buzzer off. He rose slowly from the bed and went to the bathroom, returning shortly after doing his morning ablations. Upon returning to the bed, he gently helped his wife rise from the bed, walked her to the bathroom, and helped her onto the toilet.

She looked up at Tim gratefully. "For better or for worse," she murmured, "this is the last time you'll have to do that, Tim."

"Yes, Hanna, but I would do it for a hundred years without complaint."

"I know you would, honey. I love you all the more for it."

"Are you all right here? I was going to go down and make breakfast."

"I'm fine, dear. I can't eat anything today, of course, just make something for yourself."

"That's right, I forgot. Maybe I won't have anything; I think I'm too nervous to eat."

"You should eat something. It's going to be a long day for you."

"I know, but I can always pick up something at the hospital."

"I'll finish up here. My legs are steady enough. Make yourself some coffee and toast, please. By then I should be done and you can help me get dressed and bring me downstairs."

"Ok, dear. You sure you feel strong enough?"

"Yes, Hon. My muscles are fine, it's just that my brain won't tell them to work, that's all. I'll be able to stand and face the sink. I'll be good standing there."

"Ok, I'll be back in a few minutes."

Hanna finished on the toilet, struggled to her feet and turned and leaned on the sink, washing her face for the last time. The doctor told her not to wear makeup or jewelry. She looked at her face in the mirror and thought "Will I still see this plain woman in the mirror when I wake up in rehab? Will she still be me? Will 'I' still be 'me'?"

She finished her washing just as Tim came back upstairs.

"Ready, my love?"

"Yes, Hon." As Tim helped his beloved walk out of the bathroom and back into the bedroom to change, she commented ruefully, "After all these years, I still don't know what you saw in me. I feel so plain."

"God told me you were the one for me. I don't think I ever had a chance. I was smitten from the moment I saw you."

Hanna smiled with a fleeting bit of happiness. "I bet you tell that to all the girls."

"No, only the ones I marry and spend fifteen years with."

"That many?" Tim walked her to the side of the bed and helped her sit.

"What outfit do you think I should wear?" she asked plaintively. "I know the doctor said it should be something simple, but I can't make up my mind between the blue outfit or the green one."

"I think the blue one is better on you. Besides you won't need it that long."

"I know, but I really don't want to look plain on my last day on earth."

"Darling, it's not your last day. You'll probably outlive me by several hundred years! You'll be around for as long as you like!"

She looked at Tim and smiled wistfully.

Tim tenderly assisted Hanna to get dressed in her blue outfit, then he quickly finished dressing. He helped her down the stairs where at the base of the stairs waited a treaded motorized chair.

The chair was semi-autonomous and when it sensed Hanna getting close, it lifted itself to help her seat herself, being tuned to her brain through implants that had been previously embedded to assist her mobility. She didn't really drive the motorized chair, as much as visualize the location of where she wanted it to take her.

"Before we leave, Hon, step into the living room with me and let us pray one last time together before we leave," Tim said quickly.

"Of course, darling."

She rolled into the living room and Tim stood before her and knelt. He took her hands into his and they both closed their eyes.

Tim began, "In the name of God the Father, and His Son our Saviour Jesus Christ, we pray to you. Dear Father, our dear Hanna, who has blessed me with over fifteen years of wedded bliss is about to embark on a perilous journey today. We pray in Jesus' name that you guide her surgeon's hand with strength and courage and you return her safe to us this day. We pray that each doctor and each assistant is refreshed and at his or her own best today. Allow them to focus fully on the task at hand and may each decision be correct and each procedure accurate. Amen."

Hanna then added, "Dear Lord, your Son, Jesus Christ is my personal Savior and I place myself in his hands today. Please allow my doctor to be accurate and true. And, my Lord, my sweet loving Lord, should you decide that I must be with you today and no longer on this Earth as I have been, please watch over my loving husband, Tim. I never deserved such a loving and caring man. Please take care of him, the only man I have ever loved. Amen."

Tim looked up at her with tears in his eyes. "My darling, I will be with you when you awake from your surgery in VR rehab. I will always be by your side, you know that. But, are you certain, my dear, that you want to go through with this?"

"Yes, I don't fear the consciousness transcription. The clinic has given me so much information and I have full confidence in the doctor. It's probably going to be more tiresome than anything else. I'll just be lying there while everyone else does the work."

"No, I meant, are you sure you want to go through the transcription itself? You and I differ so much on this, for this seems so much against God's plan for man. What will happen to your soul? Will your soul and body be separated?"

"Tim, we've talked more than enough about this," Hanna assured him. "It's just like my chair is a prosthesis for my legs, I'll be getting a prosthetic brain, that's all. I'm sure my soul will still reside in me, wherever I am."

"This is still such a radical procedure. It's still quite controversial. The courts are still deciding the issues. You could be considered not human any longer. You might even be considered legally dead!"

"Tim, yes, it's still quite controversial but really it's the only option open to me, you know that. Besides, I don't care what the courts decide, I'll still know I'm me and that I'm human. I'm not turning into a robot!"

With no further words, the two then proceeded to the hospital in the early morning dawn.

At the hospital, after Hanna checked in at admissions, they sat impatiently in the waiting area. Hanna was in her motorized chair and Tim sat next to her. After about twenty minutes, the surgeon, who was also Transcribed, rolled up to them.

"Hanna, how are you feeling today?" he asked.

Hanna looked at him with just a bit of fear cracking through her stoic appearance.

"I'm a bit nervous, Doctor."

"That's to be expected, of course. But are you feeling well, do you have any additional symptoms or other issues?"

"No, Doctor. I feel fine. I just want to get this over with. I've thought about nothing else for months. I want to get on with my life, even if it is inside a box." Feeling embarrassed by her statement, she looked at the Doctor and said, "I'm sorry, I didn't mean to…"

"It's no problem, Hanna, really. Yes, life does go on, but it does change. But really that is what life is all about, isn't it? We are constantly changing. Often slowly, but sometimes it is very quickly. But we change. As they say, the only constant, is change."

"Thank you Doctor," said Hanna.

The surgeon then turned to Tim.

"Father, are there any questions I can answer for you?"

"No, Doctor. My wife and I have prayed about this often and while I have my reservations, I want the best for my Hanna."

"Have you had a chance to go to any of the counseling groups we talked about?"

"No, Doctor, I have spoken to a much greater Counselor, my God and my Bible. I gain solace from them."

"Very well, Father. If you have any questions, please reach out to the social services group here. They'll be able to answer any of your questions."

The Doctor then turned back to Hanna.

"Well, Hanna, shall we go? There is a bit of preparation you have to go through before we start. And I have to mate to the surgical suite. If you are ready, why don't you follow me?"

"One moment, Doctor."

Hanna then wheeled her chair in front of Tim. She leaned over and they embraced and kissed.

She held Tim's face and said, "Be well, my darling. I will see you soon."

"You as well, my love. God is with you now."

They hugged one last time then she turned and followed the Doctor through the doors to surgery.

Tim sat back down to wait.

Several hours later, as Tim sat alone in the waiting room, the surgeon rolled up to Tim.

"Father Misinger, would you come with me please?"

"Doctor, is there a problem?"

"Please come with me," was the surgeon's non-answer. Tim followed him silently into a nearby office and sat on one of the chairs.

The Transcribed surgeon rolled up next to him.

"I'm sorry, Tim. There was nothing we could do. Her instantiation failed. There was some initial activity, but we could not..."

"What do you mean? You mean she's gone?"

After a pause the doctor said, "Yes. The transcription was proceeding normally when we encountered trouble. Instead of a conscious transcription we were forced to use an unconscious transcription method to try to salvage as much as possible from her brain. The cancer was too advanced. Too much of her brain had been destroyed; we really couldn't recover enough matter to make her sensate. She never instantiated, she never regained consciousness. She was passed peacefully."

His face darkens and he turned to the surgeon angrily, "How could you know that, robot?"

"Please Father, there is no need to use that tone of voice. Please understand..."

"Understand? Of course I understand! You failed her! She put her faith in you instead of God and you tortured and de-filed her!"

"Please, Father Misinger, she felt no pain, I assure you!"

"Of course she felt pain! How could she not feel pain as she watched her body be defiled by those infernal machines! I begged her to let God take her silently and without pain and let the mercy of God proceed according to His plan. But she was insistent. She refused to opt-out. She actively sought out you monsters!"

The surgeon remains expressionless, "Father, I'll leave you now. Please contact me if you have any questions. You may stay here as long as you need. Someone from Social Services will contact you about her remains. I'll look in on you in a little while."

The surgeon left the office and Father Misinger wept despairingly, looking up at the ceiling as if trying to see beyond its walls.

"God, why are You punishing me like this?" he cried. "I prayed for her soul. I prayed for Your forgiveness. I prayed for Hanna's delivery from the disease YOU sent her. Why have You turned against me? Why have You forsaken me? How can I go on now without my darling wife?"

CHAPTER 1
THE INTERVIEW

Charles Stevens for WIRED
August 2175

When I was first approached to interview Father Ralph Chalmers, head of the First Church of the Transcribed, I was initially hesitant. I had heard about the church and thought it was some sort of gimmick. I thought the story of Father Chalmers' miraculous revival was more smoke and mirrors than actual fact. Also I felt that it was somehow a ruse to fleece the unwary of their earnings. Enough storefront preachers have tried this before, although not with such a technological bent as this. I was not interested in writing an exposé on a subject such as this at the time. I felt that if it was a trick, it would be found out soon enough. These kinds of scams rarely stand the test of time.

My editor prevailed upon me to do more investigations and see if there was enough meat here to do an interview. She said that if I thought it didn't smell right, she would back off, although she had heard from some of her friends that there was something unique here.

Over the last decade as costs have started to come down and technology has incrementally been improving, brain transcriptions have started to become more accepted by society. Though even now there is still some hostility to the Transcribed. Certain religious people claim that there can be no soul transferred as part of the process, so even though the Transcribed is a legal individual, they are nothing but soulless machines. They are just sophisticated computer programs that mimic the personality of the deceased.

By anyone's standards, the prospect is terrifying and only performed as a last resort when the death of the body cannot be avoided by any other means. The brain, the essence, is moved to a computer. Actually a computing substrate composed of millions of other computers that replicate the functions of the replaced brain. Dendrite by dendrite, each neuron is replaced with a nano-sized quantum computer that totally replicates the source brain cell. But to do this movement from flesh and blood to silicon, the neuron is destroyed. So the process is one of movement, not copying. We don't end up with two brains. Once the brain is completely Transcribed, what is left is so much hamburger. Utterly and completely destroyed in the process of transcription. The body is decimated as well, since the process must also dig out the major nerves from the spine and extremities.

Father Chalmers' story of his transcription is incredible by anyone's standard. His body was killed in a car accident and his body lay dead for at least three hours before starting the transcription process. By any medical definition he was about as dead as he could ever be. His brain supposedly had no neural activity for at least fifteen minutes and according to the medical personnel I asked, his brain would have decayed in the time so that transcription would have been impossible. The synapses between his neurons would have decayed so much that there wouldn't have been a viable personality to activate in the computing platform.

Additionally, he shouldn't have had the transcription attempted in the first place. Both he and his wife had opted out of transcription preferring death to an afterlife inside a computer. And yet his wife overrode his wishes and demanded the transcription attempt over the recommendations of all medical and technological staff.

Though now divorced both he and his ex-wife say now that it was the correct thing to do.

I contacted Father Chalmers and asked if he would be open

to an interview. He agreed and invited me to one of their services in their church. He gave me the address and I made an appointment to see him following one of his services.

The location turned out to be a rather plain looking converted warehouse. I had envisioned a cathedral with the priests in white bodies and robes. Everything painted white, white treads, white oculars, white everything. Perhaps even with a fog machine creating clouds giving the illusion of being transported to heaven. But that was not the case. There were no apparent trappings that you would find in other cathedrals. No icons, crucifixes, not even a choir or organ, or anything of a religious nature.

In fact, the space was completely open. There was no altar or sacristy. The Transcribed walk, trundle, and roll up forming neat rows. There are no pews, they simply stand or park.

These are the flock of the Transcribed. Those that took to being moved to a processing substrate, but did not give up the feeling of having a soul. Their faith is undeterred. Some say they feel closer to God now, than they did when they were embodied in flesh.

For them there is no wine, no host, and no physicality of transubstantiation.

I did watch the service, but for the unTranscribed or otherwise enhanced, there was nothing to see. All communication is performed in VR (Virtual Reality). To the unaided, it just appears as if a bunch of machines are standing around, waiting.

I was provided with a VR helmet by one of the church's human acolytes to observe the service. It was visual/audio only with no tactile interface. I was told that there are additional channels that could be made available, but they did not have the resources to provide them. Only if I came in with my own VR setup or was Transcribed, could I experience the totality of the service.

In the VR world was the cathedral I had imagined. I donned the helmet and could see the Transcribed superimposed on my vision. All around was a grand space. And more interestingly, the Transcribed did not present themselves as their robot bodies, but the flesh and blood bodies that they had before they were Transcribed. I have been told that maintaining a pre-deceased body image is helpful in manipulating their robot bodies. I have no idea how they envision themselves as they reside within the physical structure of their bodies. Perhaps they think of themselves driving a tank or other wheeled/treaded vehicle as they make their way through the physical world.

The service itself actually felt like more of a traditional service. It had a Christian flavor to it, which relates to Father Chalmers' upbringing. That is where I saw and heard the choir. Father Chalmers led the service and in his sermon spoke about universal truths and quantum consciousness.

However, the actual communion was unavailable to me as I was untranscribed. I could not participate in the high bandwidth link that was the object of the service. This high-speed communion is similar to the communion in physical religious services. Through this process the minister connects the communicants with God. On the physical, human plane, it is done through the transubstantiation of bread and wine. Here it was the exchange of electrons in a world composed of qubits.

To my visual presentation through the helmet, the communicants and Father Chalmers became indistinct as though viewed through a smudged lens. There appeared to be movement of some kind but I could not discern what was being moved.

Then it stopped and everyone returned to distinct clarity. Shortly after that, the service ended and the Transcribed left, both in the VR and physical world. When I took off the helmet, the space was empty with the exception of Father Chalmers and myself.

Following the service, I sat down with Father Ralph Chalmers who told me about the Church of the Transcribed.

CS: "Father Chalmers, when did you move to a computer?"

Father Chalmers: "I was transcribed eight years ago after my car accident. I had standing instructions that if I could not speak for myself, I wasn't to be transcribed in the event of my death."

CS: "Then why were you Transcribed?"

FrC: "My wife, Emily, over-rode my wishes. When we came up with our power of attorney statements she thought I meant my instructions for when we had grown old together and one of us had passed on. She was so distraught by the horrific nature of the accident, that she couldn't bear to let me go."

CS: "What happened when you woke up in VR rehab?"

FrC: "Perhaps I should speak of what happened *before* I woke up."

CS: "Very well, what happened before you woke up? I know that you've made some pretty extreme claims. However, others who have been through this type of transcription say they were unconscious and had no knowledge of what was going on."

FrC: "That may be true for others, but for me, I experienced God. I went to heaven."

CS: "Others would say you hallucinated."

FrC: "No, that is exactly what I *don't* mean. I remember the crash. It seemed to happen in slow motion. I saw the car crumple as it skidded on the highway. The autopilot was desperately trying to correct the skid. I felt my body hit the dashboard as the airbags deployed. I could feel my bones breaking deep within my body. I felt a lightness in myself and I left my body. I saw my body trapped in the car as though from a great height. Then, everything faded and there was darkness. I knew that I was dead. I could feel the darkness almost as a physical thing. I thought that somehow I had damaged myself so badly that I was blind and without sensation. I wasn't in any pain; I was just waiting for the end. Then there was light; an all encompassing light and warmth that I had never experienced before or since. I felt His infinite love wash over me as a pebble in a tsunami. I knew this was God, the Infinite."

CS: "Did God speak to you?"

FrC: "Not 'speak' as I am speaking to you, no. It seemed like his words just appeared in my mind. When I spoke to Him, it was a similar process. I would formulate my question or statement and just as I was about to speak, the words were taken from my mind."

CS: "You speak of God with the male pronoun. Is God male?"

FrC: "Heavens no! God cannot be put in a box. God transcends all. He is neither male nor female and simultaneously both. I use the male pronoun as a convenience to others."

CS: "What did you say to Him? What did he say to you?"

FrC: "It seemed like the conversation went on for hours, but I had no experience of time passing. We talked about my life and all the things I had done, and what I left undone. My transgressions, my sins, and my accomplishments. Nothing was held back. He knew me better than I knew myself. I confessed to everything. I felt like a worm."

CS: "Then what happened?"

FrC: "I remember the last exchange between God and myself. I was ready for hell, I felt unworthy of such deep unconditional love. Then God spoke to me one last time."

CS: "What did he say?"

FrC: "He said, 'My child, your greatest task lies before you. Part of my flock is cut off from me. I want you to be my good shepherd and return them to my love.' I asked, 'Lord, who is cut off? Whom do you want me to seek?' And He said, 'The Transcribed are souls lost in the wilderness. Return them to me."

CS: "What did he mean, 'return them to me'?"

FrC: "He didn't say. I presumed he meant that I should tell them that God is still there for them and they should have a church to go to."

CS: "Do you remember anything after that?"

FrC: "The next thing I knew I was reinitializing in VR Rehab."

CS: "I'm sorry, I'm unfamiliar with the term 'instantiating'. What does that mean?"

FrC: "Instantiation is the process of initialization. It was when my computer started running the program that is my mind. In the early days of computers, people would call it 'boot-up'"

CS: "Thank you.

What was your religious upbringing? Did you have any?"

FrC: "Yes I did. Both my parents were Catholics, though not strict. We were what you would call "one hour Christians". We came to church on Sunday and major holidays like Easter and Christmas, but otherwise did not have a lot of involvement with the church. But I pretty much stopped going to church after I grew up and got married. We only started going back to church after Emily got pregnant. We wanted to have our child, Christine, baptized because our parents insisted on it."

CS: "How old was your daughter when the accident occurred?"

FrC: "She was about three years old."

CS: "What did she think of your transcription?"

FrC: "At first she was confused. For some reason she thought I had gone on a trip overseas and that I was videoing to her. It got even more confusing after I came back home in my autonomous chassis. For some reason she thought I had gone to Tokyo."

CS: "Why was that?"

FrC: "To this day we don't know. Even she doesn't know. It might have been that the chassis came from Toyo-Kogyo. It had a stylized Japanese ideogram for a logo. But truly we don't know."

CS: "Did she ever visit you in VR?"

FrC: "Yes, a few times, but only basic VR. She was too young to visit in FIVR. Eventually she came to understand that daddy was in an accident and he would be going around in a robot suit from then on."

CS: "Was she sad about you being Transcribed?"

FrC: "We talked about it often with her. Also she had counseling to help her understand that I really was the same person I always was, just wearing different body."

CS: "What does she think about it now?"

FrC: "As she grew older, she met other children whose parents or significant others were Transcribed. So she is pretty good with it now. And she spends every other weekend with me as part of our visitation plan so she is around a lot of Transcribed people now. She hardly thinks anything of it really. Though now with the church that her mother goes to has a completely opposite opinion of the Transcribed so I guess you could say she sees both ends of the spectrum."

CS: "Your service seems to be Christian based rather than some other form of religion such as Islam."

FrC: "Yes. I've always felt that I should work with what I know."

CS: "So God didn't tell you to make it one sort of church or provide you with plans of how to worship?"

FrC: "Oh, mercy, no! God, as I experienced Him, is indefinable to our poor ape brains so a church is incapable of being able to define God as Muslim, Jewish, or any other form of religion."

CS: "So why the VR cathedral with the heavenly choir and gold trappings and such?"

FrC: "It is my way of trying to communicate what I felt while I was in heaven. It was nothing like it, of course, but it helps to set the tone and flavor of the service."

CS: "I've spoken to the doctors that extracted your body and Transcribed your mind. They claim that you should have had no sensation whatsoever following the crash. Your neck and spine had been broken in several places, you had serious skull fractures, and various other major contusions, any of which would have caused death instantaneously. You were dead on the scene.

The surgeon who oversaw your transcription could not detect any sign of neural activity as your neurons were Transcribed. The software should not have been able to boot your mind. There was no overt electrical activity of any sort. It was a miracle that you survived the transcription process at all. How do you explain what you claim to have experienced, when the most learned of doctors, several of whom are themselves Transcribed, say that you should not have had any experience at all?"

FrC: "That's just it, I don't have an explanation. It defies explanation; it needs no explanation. It just is. That's the amazing thing about faith, isn't it?"

CS: "There are those who would label you a heretic and charlatan. That you are preying on the weak, that you seek some advantage over those you minister. More darkly, that you are forming an army to unleash hatred and violence among the unTranscribed."

FrC: "As Transcribed people, we have no need of food, or worldly goods. We survive on electricity that our bodies create from internal piles, which can be charged by free sunlight. My ministers and I require nothing from our flock, but simply wish for them to see the love of God in His infinitude. We go amongst the Transcribed offering our services freely and without expectation of remuneration. We invite them to come to temple. They may stay or leave at their leisure. We are still individuals, we hold no ill will to any living thing."

CS: "How did you feel when you woke up in rehab knowing that your instructions had been violated by your wife?"

FrC: "For an instant, I was furious at Emily. How could she take away my death like that? How could she be so arrogant and selfish? Then I recalled my discussion with God. Then I realized she had actually done God's work. At that moment, I became grateful to her."

CS: "Why was that?"

FrC: "How could I minister to the Transcribed without being Transcribed myself?"

CS: "But you are no longer married to your wife."

FrC: "No, I am not. We divorced a year or so after I came out of rehab and took on my new body."

CS: "Why was that?"

FrC: "Overall it was probably for the same reason that other couples divorce when one of the partners are Transcribed. I could no longer fulfill her needs as a flesh and blood husband. I could hug her and touch her, but all she felt was cold metal. We parted amicably enough."

CS: "She said you were spending too much time creating your temple."

FrC: "It's not 'my temple', it belongs to all. Also, as I have no need to sleep, I would work throughout the night. I had no intension of shutting her out of my life."

CS: "She claimed you were obsessed."

FrC: "To the unTranscribed, it could appear like that. Without need of food or sleep, we can work tirelessly. Additionally since we are untroubled by hormones or other chemicals, we don't get bored or burned out or are susceptible to other frailties of the flesh."

CS: "When you were Transcribed, you had not previously chosen a body style because you had originally opted out of transition. What thoughts did you have about your choices at the time?"

FrC: "Initially I gave considerable thought to having a high end humanoid body. They utilize the latest in natural looking skin that is as sensitive to touch as a human body. But once I realized the upfront costs of such a model would be as high as a buying a house, I scaled back my selection quite a bit."

CS: "Why was that?"

FrC: "Well jokes about Star Trek and Data aside, it was

simple economics. The insurance would only cover the most minimal autonomous body style. Everything higher than that would have to be paid out of pocket. While we had savings between my wife and myself, I felt it extremely selfish to raid those savings just for myself."

CS: "Why are the upfront costs so high?"

FrC: "The costs have to do with the customization required to build the body, modify the computing hardware to fit in the body and then train the Transcribed in the use of their new abode."

CS: "Why is there so much customization?"

FrC: "To a great extent, each brain is unique and the software that actually runs the mind that is the software of the brain has to be customized on the fly by the surgeon that supervises the transcription. While each brain has a visual cortex, for example, how it actually works at a dendrite level is a combination of the way the brain is born and it's subsequent experiences. The visual cortex performs a huge amount of processing to interpret the visual images that are presented to it through the eyes. So the visual cortex has to be able to tell the difference between a tree and a broom. This interpretation is a learned process and each person learns differently. As a result, the visual information stored within the visual cortex is unique. That uniqueness has to be preserved as it is Transcribed from human neuron to computing hardware.

And then there is the training the Transcribed has to do in order to learn how to use the new body. Also, the closer a body is to a humanoid form, the smaller the volume to put the computing hardware. A Body on Treads, or BoT, can be any arbitrary size as long as it can work within the constraints of society. A humanoid has limited internal volume for computing hardware, energy storage and support equipment. Plus it must have much more efficient effectors for arms and legs to stand upright and balance and walk.

All of these contribute to the upfront costs. The ongoing mortgage of the body usually extends decades. This covers payment for the body, insurance and recovery, and property taxes. Maintenance and upgrades are borne by the Transcribed."

CS: "Why is the process called transcription?"

FrC: "Well, there really isn't a better word for it in English. What would you call the process of moving the essence of your brain, your brain program, from one computer to another?"

CS: "Can't the brain just be copied? Aren't the Transcribed just a copy of the brain?"

FrC: "The human brain cannot be copied, it can only be Transcribed. What is left after the operation are lifeless cells. It is impossible to copy a living human brain."

CS: "Why is that?"

FrC: "The only way the brain could be reliably copied is if all cells and all components could be copied instantly."

CS: "I don't understand."

FrC: "The process of copying that is done today is the same, whether you are tracing a copy of a picture with paper and tracing paper, running it through a copying machine, or making a copy of a program on a computer.

The process is sequential. Each part that is copied is examined one at a time and is duplicated on the copy medium. The human brain is a dynamic system and is constantly in flux. A sequential method of copying would mean that no matter how fast you copied each dendrite and each neuron, from the time you started the process to the time you finished, the state of the total brain would have changed. The copy would not be an exact duplicate of the original.

That is the reason the legal point that allows the Transcribed to be considered the same person as they were before."

CS: "Why is that?"

FrC: "This is where we get into the vagaries of the philosophy of what it is to be human and the "Ship of Theseus" paradox."

CS: "Meaning what, exactly?"

FrC: "It is a thought experiment that goes all the way back to Crete. The ship of Theseus was preserved by the Athenians. When a part became decayed, it was replaced with one that was exactly the same as the one being replaced. Eventually, after many years, the entire ship, every plank, every oar, and every sail was replaced. So was the ship of Theseus the same as the original or was it different?

In the case of the Transcribed, there is a corollary statement. What if, instead of a wooden plank that was replaced, what if you replaced the plank with an exact copy, but it was made out of steel? The steel would be very strong and last much longer, but it wasn't wood. Is the ship of Theseus still the same ship if all the planks had been replaced with steel?"

CS: "So how does that differ from having your brain copied?"

FrC: "The original brain does not exist when the process is completed. Each cell in the brain is replaced with an identical cell that behaves exactly as the one removed. However this new cell is a quantum-based nano-computer. It behaves exactly as the cell it replaced but now it is much more durable. Just like the steel plank in the Ship of Theseus.

The legal argument was that you couldn't point to a single element of a human and say that component is human, but all the rest are not human. It is the totality of the human that makes a human. Even if that human no longer contains any parts made of flesh."

CS: "So is that why self-aware AI's can't be considered human, legally? Even though they are self-aware and can pass Turing tests?"

FrC: "Yes, that is the point. It's that the Transcribed started out as human, which makes the legal definition. Self-aware AI's were never human to begin with so they cannot have any legal claim of humanity. Though personally, I think that is an overly restrictive definition and our church is working with legal advocates and SAI's to help them gain legal status."

CS: "I kind of understand. But I'm still not clear on the definition of a human."

FrC: "Let me give a different example. If a person has an accident and his foot is destroyed and it is replaced, is that person any less of a human? Have they lost a foot's worth of humanity?"

CS: "Of course not."

FrC: "Continue the analogy. Replace every part of a human and where does that person stop being a human? Legs, arms, every organ of the body can now be replaced either with a mechanical equivalent or one cloned from their own body. They are considered no less human for having a replacement than when they were born.

This is just extended to mean the components of the brain."

CS: "But once you are Transcribed, can't the individual computers that make up your new brain be copied to a second brain and leave the original Transcribed brain?"

FrC: "No, each computing element that makes up my brain is a quantum computer, just like a neuron. The act of copying it would destroy the state of the original. Meaning that the second computer is a transcription of the first computer, but that one is equally destroyed in the process of transcription just like the first time."

CS: "So are you saying that the soul is moved from one brain to another in transcription? That each neuron and dendrite is a quantum computer? And the soul exists in the brain?"

FrC: "I cannot know where the soul resides. Early on it was thought that the soul resided in the heart, then the head. By your statement that would imply that the soul resides in the brain. God is the One who bestows souls on humanity, so it is He that would say where the soul resides. All I can say is that when I died, I met God and He set me on the path."

CS: "What is the legal status of a Transcribed while they are in rehab?"

FrC: "When a person is initially Transcribed they are in a grey area legally where they are only provisionally considered legally alive. The Transcribed is issued a temporary transcription license that allows them to continue to make independent legal and financial decisions. These allow the Transcribed to continue paying their bills, for example, and entering into certain legal contracts, such as the mortgage on their chassis. However the licenses could be rescinded by state and federal agencies if the Transcribed is deemed not to be viable."

CS: "What could cause a self-aware transcription be deemed not viable?"

FrC: "The most obvious case is when the software cannot run the software of the Transcribed mind. Usually that occurs at the initial boot time. But the Transcribed is tested throughout the rehab period to ensure that the legal individual that inhabited the flesh and blood body has been successfully Transcribed to the computing hardware."

CS: "That sounds invasive. What are some of the tests that are performed?"

FrC: "Most of the testing involves memory and the re-call of events of their life, but there are additional tests that ensure that the Transcribed mind is running correctly on the computing substrate."

CS: "How are memories tested?"

FrC: "There are empirical tests that are basically checksum tests between the memories that were contained within the flesh and blood brain and the Transcribed stored memories."

CS: "What about the functionality tests?"

FrC: "Those have to do with ensuring that the Transcribed

mind is functioning as well as it was when it was embodied in flesh. In other words making sure that the Transcribed doesn't come out as a psychotic or otherwise psychologically damaged."

CS: "That sounds like an inquisition."

FrC: "Some say it is. Basically the Transcribed has to prove that they are as sane and normal as when they were flesh."

CS: "What happens if they fail the tests?"

FrC: "They are terminated. Their software is stopped, their computing hardware is reformatted and all copies of their Transcribed software is erased. They are truly dead."

CS: "Does that happen often?"

FrC: "The current rate is less than .01 percent. The transcription process is very good."

CS: "But because of that less than one tenth of one percent chance, you chose not to discuss your experiences with God while in rehab. You only spoke of them after you had been certified as a legal individual with a permanent transcription certification. Why is that?"

FrC: "I was fearful that I could be declared a failed transcription. I don't think that is what God had planned for me. So I decided to withhold any discussion about my experience or my memories of the experience until I was out of rehab."

CS: "Weren't you afraid that the memories would be picked up by the checksum tests?"

FrC: "Yes, I was, but my flesh brain had been so damaged by the accident that they could not checksum the memories with a high degree of confidence. As a result I was under heightened scrutiny and review before I was certified."

CS: "What did that scrutiny entail?"

FrC: "I was interrogated to review my memories and they were compared to others recollection of shared events. Mostly from my wife, but my boss, co-workers, and family members also had to submit depositions."

CS: "Since you are here, I assumed you passed. (laughs)"

FrC: "(laughs) Yes, I did make it, but there was a certain fear in all of it."

CS: "Did you start thinking about your temple while you were in rehab?"

FrC: "No, but I was thinking about how I would spread the Word of God to the Transcribed when I came out of rehab. I didn't have a specific plan, but I knew what I was meant to do."

CS: "How long were you in rehab?"

FrC: "Subjectively, it was several weeks, but a large part of that was at over clock speeds, so by wall clock time it was just a few days."

CS: "Tell me about meeting your wife, Emily, in FIVR."

FrC: "It was soon after my computing hardware initialized. Subjectively it was a couple of days, but in real time it was just couple of hours. I awoke in an image of a hospital bed and I was confused and frightened, more frightened than I had ever been. It took me a while to realize what happened and to come to terms with the terrible changes that had occurred to me.

After a day or so, I felt composed enough to meet Emily in FIVR.

When they cross-connected me to the shared VR, I was astounded at the completeness of the simulation. I could feel the wind on my skin and smell the dandelions. There were birds chirping in the trees and clouds in the sky. I was lying on the hill, naked, staring up at the clouds when she called to me.

I turned my head and saw her and she was walking toward me. She was naked as well and we ran to each other and hugged. We hugged and I could feel her ribs under her skin. She nestled against me as she always had and she started weeping. I just kept telling her it was all right and that everything was fine.

We talked for hours about what happened and what our options were. One of the things we talked about was the body.

Emily wanted me back as much as possible in my old form. They could customize the humanoid appearance so that I had the same face and body as my flesh and blood body. But I was adamant that I wouldn't destroy our saving just to get a humanoid body. I would learn to deal with a BoT body. And maybe some day later get a body upgrade."

CS: "Did you try to tell her about your experiences?"

FrC: "I alluded to them, but I feared that if I vocalized them to her, I would be found out and I would be terminated."

CS: "What was rehab like?"

FrC: "Mostly I learned how to live in my new body. I refer to it as driving."

CS: "Why is that?"

FrC: "Well my method of locomotion is with treads not legs, so I had to practice moving around on treads instead of legs. Going on a level path is no problem, but navigating stairs or other inclines is more challenging. And there are some things I can no longer do, such as climb a ladder."

CS: "What about your arms and hands?"

FrC: "They operate much like my flesh and blood equivalents. I have full tactile sensation in my fingers, hands and arms. I can feel your touch from my shoulders to my fingertips. Also my hand and arm strength are similar to what I had before. The main difference here is that, of course, working out or lifting weights doesn't increase my strength, just drain my batteries. If I want more strength I just use more energy."

CS: "Are you stronger than a human?"

FrC: "I could be if I got the appropriate upgrades. Just like a man operating a backhoe is 'stronger' than a man with a shovel. But my current body is just as strong as a regular human."

CS: "So what happens at a service? Is anyone allowed to attend?"

FrC: "We meet and commune with each other. I speak of my experience meeting God and how he tasked me to bring his flock back to him. All are invited, however, we commune using a software hack of our visual cortex that allows high speed, wide bandwidth communication. The unTranscribed may participate to a certain extent using a down-convert VR bridge. However, some of the communicants may appear to speak too swiftly or communicate too deeply to understand in real time. We make the down-converted version of our service available following its conclusion, without charge."

CS: "Do you lead the service?"

FrC: "Often I do, but other within our flock have become ordained as well and they share leadership responsibilities."

CS: "Is your church expanding?"

FrC: "There has been an increase of participants over the course of our tenure. Many come for a single service and never return. All seem to be touched in some way. The Church of the Transcribed is just a few years old and we hope that it will grow more as we go forward."

CS: "How do you make yourself known to the community?"

FrC: "'I' don't make myself known. It is the church that is trying to expand its presence. Our online presence is the only advertising we do. On the site we make available recordings of our services."

CS: "You say you have other ministers and acolytes. Are there others who have communed with 'God'?"

FrC: "No. So far I am the only one."

CS: "Then how do they become ministers?"

FrC: "When we are in communion through the high band-width link, I open my mind and memories to all who are linked in. While the memories of my experience with God do not exist, my sensorium from my earliest seconds do. In them they can find the residual reflected infinite love that I was immersed in and the memories of my conversation with God. From that they can infer the presence of the Supreme Being. Part is based on faith, part on evidence. No software glitch or twiddling of my operating system could produce the aura that I felt. Through those memories they come to believe."

CS: "I was going to ask you about that. You have no experiential memories from the period where you say you were seeing God, only the memories of the experience itself. In other words, memories of memories."

FrC: "Yes, that's true. The operating system that runs the program that is now my brain only started after I was completely Transcribed. That is unlike most other transcriptions where the person's mind is Transcribed while they are still conscious and the software is already running. That ensures that the Transcribed's sensorium is preserved from the living flesh to the computing platform. Effectively moving their mind from one brain to another."

CS: "You claim that you do not require any sort of remuneration for your church. And as Transcribed individuals, you need neither money, nor food. However, there are still some operating costs involved, aren't there?"

FrC: "Yes, indeed there are. We must provide for our online presence and the sanctuary that serves as our temple and the occasional maintenance of our bodies and ongoing mortgages of our bodies."

CS: "How do you pay for those?"

FrC: "Most of the Transcribed retain their property and assets through transcription. They are still legal individuals, after all. They contribute of their own free will. We ask for nothing. Of course we accept contributions from anyone."

CS: "Do you make a profit from any of your contributions?"

FrC: "Absolutely not. All funds are directed exclusively to the ongoing maintenance and development of our physical plant and online presence. Any funds that are left over are directed to other charities that accept anonymous contributions."

CS: "Why are they anonymous transactions?"

FrC: "Quite simply, we do not wish to draw attention to ourselves as a charitable organization. We cannot, at this time, take up the mantle of charity unless we have a funding structure that specifically allows for it. Those who apply to us for charitable donations are referred to other charities that could best address their needs."

CS: "Going back to your ministers; can non-Transcribed people become ministers of the Church of the Transcribed?"

FrC: "Unfortunately, no. Or at least provisionally, no. In order to understand all that occurred to me when I was Transcribed, you must be Transcribed yourself. You cannot view my memories like you would view a movie or video. The memories themselves become part or your sensorium. You must integrate them into your persona. Even for those who are Transcribed that is a difficult task and not recommended by the software vendor of BRAIN-TRAN, TRANSCRIBEWARE, or other transcription software providers."

CS: "How much of what you do in the church is not recommended by the software vendors?"

FrC: "Well, there is the memory integration process, and the high bandwidth visual cortex hack. There are others such as sensorium sharing, though that is a minor change used by others and was not developed by the church. There are others as well, if you want a complete list, I can provide it for you."

CS: "Thank you I would like that, you can send it to me when we complete the interview. You also said 'provisionally no'. What do you mean by that?"

FrC: "Some people have such extreme brain implant augmentation that they could, conceivably, integrate with the high bandwidth visual cortex hack. Their augmentations are so severe that they are all but Transcribed already, but retain a flesh and blood brain and body. But so far no one has come to us requesting such an experiment."

CS: "You tried to share your memories with Emily in a FIVR session after rehab. How did that turn out?"

FrC: "Not well, I'm afraid. When we met, I manipulated the FIVR environment to present my memories to her; to project them into her mind. I presented them to her as the most precious of my memories. She accepted them, but afterwards, she said it just felt and looked like gibberish to her. She could not comprehend what I experienced."

CS: "How did you feel about that?"

FrC: "I was heartbroken. She couldn't seem to understand what it all meant to me and she felt I was throwing away my life for what may have only been either some random software glitch or a result of my head trauma in the accident."

CS: "There are some who say that the Transcribed are pulling away from their humanity; that they are becoming a species unto themselves. As they mature in the Transcribed environment, they have less in common with their flesh and blood lives. Do you think that is true?"

FrC: "I have to say that I am not a good representative of the greater Transcribed souls. As minister of the Church, I spend most of my time around Transcribed individuals, so my opinion might be skewed."

CS: "What about those who come to church? Do they say they feel less connected to their flesh and blood relatives and family?"

FrC: "Some do, yes. But overall, most just come to temple for the fellowship of other Transcribed through the communion of the high bandwidth link."

CS: "Thank you Father Chalmers, this concludes our interview."

FrC: "And thank you, Charles, for the opportunity to speak to you. You are welcome any time to come back and ask more questions."

CS: "Thank you, I very well may do that."

Following the interview with Father Chalmers, I had an interview with Father Chalmers former wife, Emily Chalmers. I spoke to her regarding her experiences with her former husband, Ralph, and what occurred before and after his transcription.

CS: "What can you tell me about your ex-husband, before the accident and transcription?"

Emily Chalmers: "Ralph was a wonderful husband and a good provider. We both had our own careers, of course, but he never withheld anything, he was always caring about us and our life together."

CS: "What was his career prior to the accident?"

EC: "He was an insurance adjuster. He would examine various claims and determine the necessary payouts from the insurance."

CS: "Was he good at his job?"

EC: "I think he was. His co-workers seemed to like him and occasionally we would have cook outs where we lived and invite our neighbors and our co-workers, and we all had a good time."

CS: "Was there any friction in the marriage?"

EC: "No more than I would think other couples have. We had our differences, of course, but it never got in the way of the love we had for each other."

CS: "How long had you been married?"

EC: "Seven years. We were good for each other. We made each other laugh. I remember snuggling up to him under the covers when we slept and hearing him breathe. We went to games together. He was on a softball team. I loved to watch him swing. He was so manly."

CS: "Did you have children together?"

EC: "One child, Christine. She was so young when Ralph

had his accident. It was hard for her to understand what happened to him. I felt so sorry for her. She must have felt so lonely."

CS: "Do you have children now?"

EC: "David, my current husband, and I talked about it quite often while we were dating. We haven't taken that step yet."

CS: "Tell me about the accident."

EC: "Oh God. That was one of the darkest moments of my life."

CS: "What happened?"

EC: "Ralph would spend a lot of time on the road. So many claims, with so much territory to cover. He was driving home one evening and he had the autopilot on. There had been a light rain earlier in the day. Apparently, from what they can tell, the right front tire had a blowout. The car started to skid and turn, and even with the auto-pilot trying to correct the skid, the tire threw the car off balance and it rolled over three times before coming to rest in a ditch. The car automatically called for help, of course, but it was a rural area and it took the emergency team fifteen minutes to get to him. By then he was already dead."

CS: "How were you notified?"

EC: "I received a call from the local police. They said he had been in an accident and had died. He was wearing his 'NO-TRANSCRIPTION' medallion and they wanted to verify that he wouldn't be Transcribed or revived."

CS: "You both had taken a no-transcription opt-out. Why did you override his wishes?"

EC: "To this day, I'm not really sure why I told them to take him to the hospital for transcription. What I recall is all the memories of the times we had together and realizing there wouldn't be any more of them. He would become a memory to me and I would never be able to speak to him again. I was devastated. I just knew I wanted more memories with him. Or at least to have closure."

CS: "He was airlifted from the accident to the hospital and prepared for transcription. With the recovery of his body and the airlift and the preparation, about three hours elapsed. At any point in that time, you could have called and rescinded the transcription order. Did you have any second thoughts during that time?"

EC: "Not really. All I remember is driving to the hospital. It took about an hour to drive there and while I was driving, I kept thinking about how lonely he must have felt. To die alone seemed like such a terrifying experience. I hoped that the transcription would be successful, because at the very least, I wanted to be able to say goodbye to him. To let him know that he wasn't really alone. I still loved him and would always love him."

CS: "The doctors felt that it was an unnecessarily heroic effort. Even though his body was maintained as much as possible at the accident and in transport, the odds of his persona surviving the death of his brain and body were almost near zero. The deterioration of the neural matter in the period of time he was without life support should have destroyed any vestige of his mind. They advised against the attempt, didn't they?"

EC: "Yes, they did. They said that if they were unsuccessful, there still would be a transcription charge and the co-pay for it was significant, even after insurance paid out. And by state and federal law, if the transcription were not deemed viable, all computing platforms would be invalidated and re-formatted, effectively killing whatever might have been Transcribed."

CS: "And you went ahead anyway. Despite both of you opting out of transcription and the chance of success being extremely low."

EC: "Yes. Again, I really don't know why, other than I couldn't bear to be without him."

CS: "That seems like both a very loving, but very selfish reason."

EC: "Yes, it was. I recognized it then and now. But, Charles, I'm feeling a bit persecuted by this line of questions. I'm feeling like I'm having to justify my decision. If there are going to be more questions of this nature, I will end this interview."

CS: "I'm sorry, that was not my intension. I truly like to know all parts of a story and trying to understand motivations can sometimes seem adversarial. Please accept my apologies, it is only my intension to be objective.

I do have one last question, however, in that line and realize that I'm not being adversarial by asking it and you can decline to answer."

EC: "Ok. What other questions do you have?"

CS: "Do you feel that you received any sort of encouragement to have Ralph Transcribed?"

EC: "You mean did I feel that God made me do it? That I was doing God's work as part of Ralph's 'miracle'?"

CS: "Yes, something like that. Ralph mentioned that in my interview with him."

EC: "Ralph and I talked about that and others have asked me as well. The short answer is no. I felt no 'guiding hand' or commandment from heaven to have him Transcribed. My feelings were my own and my decision was completely mine. I don't blame or thank God for what occurred, it wasn't God's decision to make, no matter what Ralph thinks."

CS: "How long was it from the time of his transcription until he was re-awakened?"

EC: "It took about twelve hours for the transcription."

CS: "Why so long? Usually a transcription takes less than six hours."

EC: "There had been so much cerebral damage from the accident. His spine had been broken in three places and there were a number of cranial contusions. The doctors had to try to repair the damage before they could attempt the transcription."

CS: "Were you able to follow the process?"

EC: "Yes, the doctors kept me informed as to how things were going. Plus I was able to watch an overview of the progress from the hospitals AI."

CS: "What was going through your mind while this was going on?"

EC: "Nothing, I was numb. I called my mother and my girlfriend and they came and sat with me. They gave me a lot of support."

CS: "Did they ask you about your decision?"

EC: "Yes, we talked about it. My mother is a bit old school and thinks transcription is at best just a talking computer program and nothing more. But she was there for me and tried to comfort me. My girlfriend just accepted and let me talk and cry it out."

CS: "Where was Christine during this time?"

EC: "I dropped her off with Ralph's parents. They were devastated by the news and wanted to do everything they could to help. Having Christine stay with them comforted them and Christine."

CS: "What happened when the transcription was complete?"

EC: "The transcription staff came to me and offered to let me be in VR when the software booted up."

CS: "Did you accept?"

EC: "Initially, I said no. From what I was told, the Transcribed awaken confused and disoriented. I didn't want to be there for that. I wanted to be there when I could talk to him rationally and calmly."

CS: "How long was that?"

EC: "By 'real' clock time, it was about two hours. Though in VR, they accelerated the clock rate, so to Ralph, it probably seemed like a few days."

CS: "Had you ever been in fully immersive VR before?"

EC: "No. I've used VR helmets before, but those only give audio and visual and minor tactile sensations. Fully immersive VR or 'FIVR' overrides all sensory input to your brain and supplants it with the VR environment. It is like being transported to another land. You can see, hear, feel, smell, and even taste in the VR world. The FIVR environment is extremely limited because of that. The 'world' is small because the number of sensations is so high. It is difficult to synchronize all those input/output streams."

CS: "Where did you meet Ralph following his re-emergence?"

EC: "I discussed that with the doctors. I thought it would be best if we met in an environment that was peaceful and calm. I chose a field of dandelions on a gentle hill."

CS: "How did Ralph react when he saw you?"

EC: "He was lying on his back staring up at the sky, he turned his head when I called to him. He stood and ran to me and we hugged. I could smell his body, I could feel his muscles. I lost myself in his embrace. I knew it was all a sham, of course. We were nothing but a bunch of qubits in a computer but it felt so very real. I started crying and I never wanted to let him go.

I couldn't stop sobbing. He lifted my face to him with his gentle hands and kissed my tears. He was consoling me, running his hand over my hair, telling me it was all right. He was back and he was here for me.

I looked up to him and he kissed me in a way that I knew it was him. He had a way of kissing me that was unique. I knew him, I knew his kiss. I felt his body. It was him."

CS: "Then what happened?"

EC: "We talked for what seemed like hours. The human brain can't be over clocked like the Transcribed, so we were in real time during that period.

My FIVR setup required me to be in bed and fully catheter-ized with an IV drip for liquids and nourishment. I could have remained in FIVR for days if needed."

CS: "How long did you spend with Ralph in FIVR?"

EC: "At that time, about a day and a half. There were a few other times after that as he worked through rehab."

CS: "What happens in VR rehab?"

EC: "The Transcribed is trained through simulation to use their new body."

CS: "Since you both had opted-out of transcription, there was no pre-selected body style was there?"

EC: "No, and we both had to discuss that at length with each other. The most humanoid style looks very naturally human, but is hideously expensive. It would have taken a hundred years to pay it off. We had to opt for one that was more affordable."

CS: "But a Transcribed has a lifetime that is indefinite in length, so wouldn't having a humanoid style body be almost as easy to afford as less costly models?"

EC: "The insurance would only pay so much of the upfront costs of a body and anything over that would have to be paid by the insured. And that would have decimated our savings. Ralph was thinking of me when he made that decision. He didn't want to use all of our money on himself. So he opted for a base model with very few enhancements."

CS: "So how did he take to rehab?"

EC: "He handled it very well. It was a challenge, but he managed it."

CS: "What sort of challenges did he have?"

EC: "Well for example, learning to walk is a challenge. He has treads now, not legs, so learning to move required different motor skills than just balancing and using his legs."

CS: "Were there other issues?"

EC: "Mostly learning his new body's height and learning not to knock things over as he moved around. Also, interpreting and integrating the robot body's signals into his sensorium. He says that when his energy storage runs low, he feels it as a kind of hunger. He doesn't need to sleep, per-se, but his mind does need periodic episodes of inactivity to integrate his short and long term memories. That is a hold over from having a human brain, it is not a function of the computing platform that runs the program of his brain."

CS: "While he was in rehab, did he talk with you about his experiences prior to being booted up?"

EC: "No, he wouldn't talk to me about it then. He alluded to it several times, but I couldn't get him to do more than just hint at something that happened 'before'."

CS: "Did he ever say why he couldn't talk about it in rehab?"

EC: "He did tell me later that he was fearful that if he talked about his experience with God, that they would say he was a failed transcription and terminate him."

CS: "Could that have happened?"

EC: "From what I understand, probably not. But I can understand how vulnerable he must have felt, since his entire existence had been reduced to a collection of qubits in a computer that was being overseen by the department of transcription. He was running under a temporary transcription license and he was only provisionally deemed a legal entity."

CS: "Wouldn't he have been under the same review after he left rehab?"

EC: "No, once a Transcribed has left rehab and inhabits an independent computing platform, their legal status as an individual is assured and they must be accorded all rights and privileges as any other human being. Any actions against them must follow due process."

CS: "So how did you feel when he spoke of his experience?"

EC: "I didn't know what to think. I still don't. In all other respects, Ralph was completely rational and as far as I could tell, the same person as he was before the accident. I thought it was some bizarre out of body experience he had as a result of the accident."

CS: "Is that what you think happened? That this was the result of the trauma he endured?"

EC: "Thinking back on it, yes. I can see no other possible explanation for what he experienced. He endured significant head trauma and anything could have happened as a result of that."

CS: "Have you attended any of the Church's services or watched their down-converted files?"

EC: "Yes I have, several times. But I cannot feel what he says he felt."

CS: "Their claim is that to truly understand the experience you must be Transcribed."

EC: "Yes, I've heard that, and I'm not about to go that far."

CS: "What happened to your relationship following Ralph's return from rehab?"

EC: "The physical change was immediate. Since he had no real reason to sleep, there was no reason to come to bed. And, of course, I couldn't really cuddle up to a bunch of steel and treads. Since he doesn't eat, we could not share meals together. I had no one to cook for, beside Christine. He would spend time with me, but the physical satisfaction of being together was lost."

CS: "What happened to his work?"

EC: "The company offered to return him to his old position or to transfer to another position at the same rate of salary."

CS: "Did he take their offer?"

EC: "He did decide to take a position that didn't require travel. He feared that the acceptance of the Transcribed is still very controversial and worried that he would be persecuted or attacked when he was out."

CS: "How long did he maintain his new position?"

EC: "Almost a year. Then he started to feel less and less enthusiastic about doing work. It was about that time that he started to have more and more contacts with other Transcribed people and talk about his experience. The other Transcribed started to take more and more of his time. Eventually he quit his job to just talk about his experiences speaking to God."

CS: "Were you upset by that?"

EC: "I was furious. He was letting something that, at best, was just a hallucination, a software glitch, take over his life and supplant the people in the real world."

CS: "How did he react to that?"

EC: "Mostly with what I would call compassionate indifference. He would sit there staring at me as I ranted and he would say nothing. Then go on as if nothing happened. When I asked him to stop, he said that he couldn't. He said he was driven to tell God's words."

CS: "So he continued to talk to others about his experience and spent less and less time with you and your daughter?"

EC: "He would stay up throughout the night, online with others. Never coming to bed. When he first came out of rehab, he would come to our bedroom and stay with me. Sometimes he would hold my hand and try to caress me as before. Of course it was different since he had a robot body, but the tenderness was still there. Then, even that stopped."

CS: "Then what happened?"

EC: "He started working with other Transcribed on their high bandwidth hack. He claimed that just sharing his thoughts online was not efficient. That too much was being lost by having to try to put into words or visual images the things he says he experienced. He wanted others to actually feel the experience, to actually be there."

CS: "Is that when he started his temple?"

EC: "No, that came later, after we divorced."

CS: "Why did you divorce him?"

EC: "I couldn't take it any longer. He was becoming more distant and uncommunicative. We just couldn't talk to each other without it becoming a fight or meaningless drivel about God."

CS: "Did you ever go back and try to be with him in FIVR?"

EC: "Only once. Going FIVR is expensive and requires medical support to care for your body while you are in VR. There's a cost associated with the Transcribed as well to cross connect his computing platform to the FIVR world. I could be with him while he was in rehab because the insurance would cover the costs. But after that it is paid out of pocket."

CS: "So what happened when you got together in FIVR?"

EC: "We met again in the field of dandelions. It was like going back before the accident. I could see him, the old him. The man I loved in the flesh. We hugged and talked. It was much more calming to my fears."

CS: "Did he talk about his experience with you then?"

EC: "Yes, he did. He also tried to merge his memory of the time with me. By using FIVR he could manipulate the environment and create the moments following his boot up. I tried to understand it all, but it just seemed like gibberish to me."

CS: "You couldn't merge his memory?"

EC: "No, I could, but to me it just seemed like random colors and sensations. From what I've been told, this is normal in a booting process as the software starts to run the mind of the Transcribed."

CS: "What happened after he tried the memory merge?"

EC: "We came back to the field and he was just staring at me, like he was expecting me to feel some rapturous joy. I just looked at him and told him that it didn't make any sense to me."

CS: "How did he react?"

EC: "He was crestfallen. Apparently he thought this would make it all better or something. He thought that if he merged his memory that I would somehow understand it all. Just the opposite, actually."

CS: "Is that when you started to think about divorce?"

EC: "It was soon after that. He seemed so obsessed with

trying to tell the Transcribed of the words of God that I felt he was turning his back on me and Christine. Before the accident we had a life together, but afterwards, he drew away from that and I had to start thinking of my own life, a life without him."

CS: "Did you have intimacies with him after the accident or while in FIVR?"

EC: "You're asking if we had sex? I refuse to answer."

CS: "Fair enough. Was the divorce amicable?"

EC: "Other than some issues about property liquidations, there really weren't any. He wanted all the property liquidated so he could start his temple, the Church of the Transcribed."

CS: "So he came up with the idea before he left?"

EC: "I presume so. By that point we were barely talking and I didn't really want to hear anything about his experiences any more or the people he was sharing it with."

CS: "What is your life like now?"

EC: "I've moved on. I've since remarried and I am happy with where I am right now."

CS: "How did you meet your current husband?"

EC: "His name is David. We met at a support group for those who have lost people close to them. Some of the people lost their loved ones because of death and others to being Transcribed."

CS: "So David lost his significant other?"

EC: "Yes, he lost his wife due to cancer. There are still some virulent forms of cancer that can't be treated through nano-meds. She succumbed in just a few months. It was heart-breaking for him."

CS: "Given what you know now and your experiences with your ex-husband, have you changed your opinion of transcription or would want to be Transcribed yourself?"

EC: "While I am much more informed about transcription and the Transcribed, I really have not changed my opinion. I would not opt for transcription were it offered and affordable."

CS: "Why is that?"

EC: "I know that the Transcribed feel themselves to be substantially the same person they were before and I wouldn't take that away from them. However, from my experiences in FIVR and talking at length with Ralph, I don't feel that a Transcribed existence is as rich as having a flesh and blood body. While they can recreate a human brain, they are still unable to put as many nerves in the Transcribed body as there are in a flesh and blood body. As a result the Transcribed is less sensitive to the world. So to me it would be like living in a cocoon and every sensation would remind yourself of what you have lost."

CS: "Don't you think that as technology improves that the richness of human existence would be more closely presented to the Transcribed?"

EC: "Yes, possibly, but it's not there now and given the snail's pace of improvement, I don't see that changing any time soon."

CS: "One final question; Does it appear to you that the Transcribed are losing their humanity and pulling away from their previous lives?"

EC: "It does to me. Through the support group I've heard story after story of how their loved one had less in common with flesh and blood people and just wanted to be with other Transcribed. Many of them have resulted in divorces like mine."

CS: "Emily, thank you for your time."

EC: "You're quite welcome."

CHAPTER 2

T he process of transcription did not appear overnight. It grew out of a continued merging of information technology and medical understanding of the mind and brain.

Artificial neurons were not a new concept. They had been mathematically defined and actually created in the early twenty-first century. However, they were all just algorithms of what was observed in actual neurons. There was no deeper concept of understanding of a neuron. It was viewed on a purely mechanical basis like a computing element called a Programmed Logic Array. A PLA is a simple device that produces a certain output based on the input it receives. If, for example, signals are received on input lines 1, 3, and 7, it may produce an output on output lines 7, 5, 9, and 12. A different configuration of input signals produces a different set of output signals. A neuron is very similar. A neuron may produce output along its axon terminals, based on whether or not it receives input from certain dendrites. The axon terminals are in turn attached to other dendrites that are attached to other neurons. Where the dendrites and axons meet there is a gap called the synapse. From a computational standpoint, substituting a PLA for a neuron appears to be a straightforward affair. Simply determine the signals from the dendrites cause the axon to fire and replace it with a functionally identical PLA.

However, deeper understanding of the neuron showed that while there was a brute force component of the neuron that had a response like a PLA, there was also a deeper component that influenced certain configurations of outputs of the axon. This deeper component was initially proposed by

Rodger Penrose and Stuart Hammeroff in the late twentieth century, as Orchestrated Objective Reduction or Orch-OR. While widely criticized, it speculated that the neuron was also governed by the quantum actuation that existed in the microtubules inside the neuron. They proposed that because of the Orch-OR nature of the neuron, no classical digital computer could ever adequately mimic a human brain. While the skeptics maintained that microtubules were an order of magnitude too large and much too warm and wet to be effectively manipulated by quantum effects, no amount of brute force computation could mimic what any observed neuron could do.

It was supposed that while microtubules may not be the component that made the neuron behave like a quantum computer, something was. And it was not until the advent of room temperature qubits based quantum computers that neuron modeling truly became a reality.

Initially done in laboratory environments using animal experiments and increasingly more complex and smaller quantum computers, larger types of brain mimicking were performed. Initially starting with insects then moving up the evolutionary ladder to mouse brains, whole sections of brains were scanned and replicated, with more and more complex quantum computer substrates.

One of the first demonstrations of partial brain replication was when a mouse who had been trained to navigate a maze to a prize of food, had its visual cortex removed, evaluated, and replicated on a quantum computing substrate. Without the visual cortex, the mouse was blind and unable to navigate the maze. When the replicated visual cortex was enabled, the mouse appeared to regain the ability to see. It correctly navigated the maze and could see, grasp, and eat, its prize of food.

This was a tremendous leap for modeling. Not only was the mouse able to see again, it could interpret its world in much the same way as it did before it had its visual cortex replaced. It could visually understand the maze, what food looked like, and coordinate paw and eye movement to grasp and eat its food. Though the wires trailing out of the back of its head to a large computer did hinder its movements somewhat.

The ability to identify neuronal activity and replicate it became more and more advanced, until the time it was able to completely scan a whole mouse brain and replicate it in quantum computing substrates. A mouse without a physical flesh and blood brain effectively continued its existence in the real world through brain replication. All movement, visual acuity, and natural and trained responses were completely and successfully replicated in a computer. Additionally, the mouse continued to learn new tasks as well. Eventually, the mouse was instantiated in VR and exists to this day running on one of the oldest computational substrates. It is regularly visited by the newly Transcribed to provide an inspiration that life goes on.

All attempts to perform similar replications using classic, non-quantum based, digital computers failed. Thus it became apparent that while the actual process of quantum computing could not be adequately explained by examination of the neuron, it existed nevertheless.

The process of replication continued with more and more complex organisms being partially and wholly replicated to custom quantum computing substrates. Attempts were made to replicate neuronal activity of families of neurons, hoping to reduce the overall count of computational elements. These proved to be inadequate for more than a few neurons. Apparently, only one-to-one neuron to computer element truly replicated the complete functions of the Transcribed brain.

For a very long time, technology and medical science had worked hand in hand to create ever more powerful diagnostic and therapeutic tools. It made a major leap with the development of a line of quantum based computer neurons. They were used as a diagnostic and repair tool to correct problems within the human body. Initially they were used to replace damaged nerves within the extremities of the human body. People with broken spines were returned to full activity. People who had lost sensation due to disease or injury were given their sense of touch. One of the most profound improvements was the elimination of blindness due to retinal damage from diseases such as macular degeneration. Eventually, all blindness caused by any sort of physical injury or disease to the eye was overcome as a result of quantum retinal neuron replacements.

Human experimentation of quantum neuron replacement within the brain was begun in the early twenty-second century with the successful replication of the human auditory and visual senses.

The one issue in these replications that could not be overcome was the element of size. Quantum computing elements could not effectively be reduced in size to equivalent flesh and blood neurons. In these replications, the quantum devices were installed in helmets or vests that the person could wear and the interface to the brain was accomplished through an exterior smart plug that could attach the computing device to the overridden nerve endings.

Of course when the helmet or vest was removed, the person became blind or deaf.

Similar advances also occurred with the replication of the human cerebellum, primary motor, and Broca's area.

It was at this point that the medical, ethical, and legal disciplines came into opposition.

It was widely anticipated that eventually it would be possible to replicate all components of the human brain, including the pre-frontal cortex, which has been long considered the seat of consciousness. Ethically then, at what legal point did the replication of a brain transcend from simple repair of cerebral damage to actual replication of a thinking individual in a computing device?

So began the 'Ship of Theseus' movement. The 'Ship of Theseus' paradox is most notably recorded by Plutarch. Plutarch asked simply whether a ship that had been restored by replacing every single wooden part was indeed the same ship.

Adherents said that the Ship of Theseus argument was easily solved. If the ship still sailed, then it was the same ship. If no part of the old damaged Ship of Theseus could be used to create a second ship, then the original ship still existed, even if every piece was replaced with identical components. Too, if those replaced components were more durable, it was still the same ship. So if all the pieces of the Ship of Theseus were replaced with identical steel planks, it was the same ship, even if, eventually, the entire ship became steel.

The Ship of Theseus argument was eventually tested in a court of law when one Dennis Miller agreed to a whole brain replacement to save himself from death due to brain cancer. As he was a wealthy individual, this naturally resulted in an immediate court challenge. His heirs attempted to have him declared legally dead as his brain and body were destroyed as part of the replication process. Since his body and brain no longer lived, it was argued, Mr. Miller was dead. Mr. Miller and his attorneys argued that his death was greatly exaggerated as a result of the extreme medical procedure he had to endure to save him from brain cancer. He claimed to still be a viable human being with all the rights and privileges accorded therein. He could answer any question just as well after his brain replacement as he could before.

Additionally, he had legal representation during his procedure to attest that the same person came out of surgery as went in.

It was a curious sight nevertheless, when Mr. Miller, encased in a mobile support frame, was wheeled into court by technicians to testify on his own behalf. The opponents in the proceedings refused to question Mr. Miller directly since, if they did, they felt it would give credence to his claim that he was still alive, as only living humans were allowed to testify. Mr. Miller was allowed to provide evidence, provisionally, on his behalf, as a sophisticated transcription of his pre-deceased wishes. Thus giving rise to the term 'Transcribed' to the people who had been converted to silicon.

The point was hotly debated for over a decade as various points of law were debated, some all the way to the Supreme Court.

Eventually though, the process of transcription was ruled legally valid and legal guidelines were established to guarantee the fidelity of the transcription and the legal status of the person Transcribed. These were the memory checksums and evaluations performed on the Transcribed either during or immediately after their transcription. As long as these guidelines were met, the Transcribed were given complete human autonomy and all rights and privileges of due process.

As it had many times before though, society as a whole takes longer to accept a new concept than does science. Eventually, transcription became a common response to *certain extreme physical trauma. But not all people agreed with transcription and did not want to be Transcribed as a result of injury or disease. So the ability to opt-out of transcription was adopted. Many wore a "No-Transcribe" medallion to announce their wishes to emergency responders, if they could not speak for themselves.*

- Life Without A Brain, The History of Transcription - 2177

Following their divorce, Ralph had twice monthly visitation with Christine. Since he started the church, Christine would come and help with the set up of the cathedral. Since it was all software in VR, she took great pride in adding ornamentation of the church. Mostly she decided the time of day and stained glass design.

Ralph allowed her a rather free hand in her design. The other parishioners actually liked her work. The VR structure itself was designed by one of the parishioners who was an architect. But by putting it in VR, the structure could be any arbitrary design, even an impossible Escher design where gravity was optional. Most parishioners, however, preferred more traditional designs that did not detract from the spiritual fulfillment of the religious service.

Christine would occasionally serve as an acolyte in the service as well. But since she used a VR helmet to interface, she could not participate in communion using the high bandwidth link.

The parishioners were a loving and close-knit group, caring for each other's needs and supporting each other as they tried to integrate themselves in society.

Society, however, was still coming to grips with the idea of having autonomous machines have the same rights as humans. Discrimination was widespread and violence through tipping and vandalism prevalent. Thugs would sneak up on an unsuspecting Transcribed person and either beat them with steel rods or use the rods to tip them over. The chassis for the Transcribed is solidly built and usually incur little permanent damage.

On one particular Friday, Ralph headed out to Emily's house to pick up Christine for one of his visitations. He arrived at her house and announced himself to Emily's house security AI. The door let him in and he rolled into the living room where he found Emily, her husband Dave, and Christine sitting on the couch chatting with a casually dressed man.

"Ralph, this is Reverend Tim. He is the pastor at our church," said Emily.

The pastor barely glanced at Ralph and continued speaking to Emily's family.

"Em, I'm here to pick up Christine."

Tim turned to him and with undisguised disgust said "Begone, robot, before I reformat your hard drive! You have no business here with humans. Go regulate the Internet or something."

Astonished, Ralph said, "Just who do you think you are! Em, why is he here?"

"You don't have to answer to that gearbox, Emily. You are a human, this is a machine. Man was given dominion over all of earth by God and machines are made by man to serve man. Not the other way around. Tell it to leave now," Tim said.

"I am every bit a human being as anyone else, even though you seem to be trying to leave the species!"

"You're called a human because the courts of man says so. But God has the final authority over all, and you are no more a man than a toaster."

"Em, I won't stand for this, come along Chris." Ralph started to roll toward Christine.

Tim turned to Emily and said, "Are you going to let that *machine* take your daughter?"

Emily said hesitantly, "It is his weekend for visitation. The courts set it up. We agreed to it."

Tim pointed at Ralph and said, "That is an abomination and should be used by man, not pretend it is a man."

"Chris, let's go." Ralph extended a hand to reach for Christine.

Christine stood to go with Ralph but the minister stood up and grabbed her arm.

"You don't have to go with that thing, child, you are not bound by a computer."

Christine winced at the grip of the minister, "Ow, you're hurting me!"

With surprising agility, Ralph sped over to the minister and grabbed his wrist, "Let he go you stupid fuck! I'll have you arrested!"

Tim faced Ralph and he said, "Be arrested by a machine? Hardly."

"Let go of her or I'll brake your arm. I weigh over four hundred pounds. I'll roll over you and leave tread marks on your face."

The minister let go of Christine then Ralph released Tim's wrist.

The Reverend stepped away and looked at Emily and Dave. "I will not be threatened by a robot." Pointing at Christine he said, "I expect to see all three of you in church on Sunday." He then stormed out of the room.

Dave stood up and looked at Emily and Ralph "You two have visitation rights with Christine, but this is my house. I will not have violence here." Tim looked at Ralph. "Tim was my guest here and you disrupted it and insulted the minister of my church. If you can't behave in a civil manner, then you will no longer be allowed to come here."

"As I recall the minister is the one who started insulting me," said Ralph, his voice rising as his anger grew.

"Tim has been a life long friend to my family. He has very strong beliefs. And, frankly, I agree with them."

"So you and he think I'm no better than a machine?"

"He thinks the soul cannot be Transcribed, so when the

body dies, the soul is extinguished and can't be transferred to a machine."

"He is a bigot, and so are you," Ralph yelled.

"I won't have my minister insulted."

Emily stood up and faced them. "This has gone far enough. Christine, go with your father. Ralph we'll talk about this later."

Calming his emotions, Ralph said, "Ok, I'll bring her back on Sunday afternoon after services."

Dave said "Bring her back on Sunday morning or even better, Saturday night. The reverend meant all three of us to be at church."

Turning to Emily, Ralph said, "You know I can't do that! I have services too. I have both days on the weekend; this is un-announced and completely arbitrary. According to the agreement I have visitation from Friday after 7:00 to Sunday at 6:00 PM."

"I'm changing the arrangement," said Emily.

"Not without the court's permission!"

"I've contacted my lawyer. We're going to sue for complete custody," said Emily contritely.

"Did that bigot put you up to this? Em, you never were this way."

"What I do with MY daughter is MY concern."

"I'm her father and I have my rights, too!"

"We'll see about that!" Dave put in.

Turning to her daughter Emily said, "Go with your father, Christine, and we'll come get you Sunday morning."

"Em, please don't do this. Chris has been helping at the church, she likes it."

Christine said, "I don't want to go to Tim's church, it's so boring!"

"Things will be changing, Ralph. Get used to it. And Christine, you are too young to understand. This is about your spiritual wellbeing. You'll understand when you get older."

Looking down at the floor, Dave said, "You tore the rug too."

"Bill me! Come on, Chris."

Ralph is furious as he and Christine walk to the car. Ralph is surprised by his reaction and had to dial down his emotions.

"Who is that guy? I know your mom and Dave go to an evangelical church, but I didn't know it was like that," he stated.

"We've been going to his church for a while now. Dave says he's been going to that church since he was a little boy. It's boring. The service is just boring. Pastor Tim always seems so angry. He's always shouting during his sermons. I can't understand what he is talking about."

"Let's just forget that for now. Tomorrow we'll be having a picnic behind the church. I've got a couple of people coming to help prepare."

"Who all is coming?"

"Most of the congregation, and they're bringing their non-trans friends and family to help introduce them to the church. Also it will let them know that we're still human even though we're wearing different clothes."

"Yeah, metal and treads. Will there be any kids my age there?"

"A couple, I think."

"That could be fun."

"Yes."

They headed back to the church. The church was actually a converted warehouse in the industrial part of the city. Ralph purchased it with the assets from his divorce and put his life's savings into it.

It was a low rectangular two-story building with a living area in the rear upper story. It was completely open with no real appointments as a church or as a home.

The celebration of the mass was done entirely in VR so there was no need to have a physical manifestation of an altar. The Transcribed that attend had no need to sit and so there were no pews. The non-Transcribed who occasionally attended were offered folding chairs.

The service was open to all, but only the Transcribed could participate in communion. The actual participation depended on a software and hardware connection that a simple VR rig cannot provide.

During communion, the congregants attached themselves to a high-speed router and became nodes on a network. Data was shared through the optical cables attached to the router on one end, and to the Transcribed through their diagnostic plug.

The data was presented to the congregant's visual cortex through what had become to be called the "High Bandwidth Hack".

This hack allowed high speed, high bandwidth data sharing through the visual cortex. Ninety percent of a person's perception was through vision and this had become the portal by which Ralph shared his echoing encounter with God.

VR helmets could not provide access to the visual cortex in this manner as it just presents data to the eyes through miniature screens.

Even fully immersive VR, called "FIVR" could not provide the connection that was provided by the High Bandwidth hack. So for the non-Transcribed, communion was just a blur.

There was no attempt to prevent others from participating; it's just that it was physically impossible.

They arrived at the church and parked the car. The car that Ralph drove was specially modified for his larger body. The driver's seat was replaced with a fold down seat in case a human wished to drive. Normally the seat was in the retracted position so Ralph could drive. The controls were not otherwise changed. There still was a steering wheel, but acceleration and breaking were accomplished through handbrake levers attached to the steering wheel. Ralph, however, controlled the car via wireless connection to the car's AI.

Also, the car was autonomous in its own right, so it could drive without intervention to addresses given to it. Normally Ralph drove himself, because every time he got into a car, he was reminded of that awful day when he died. He was not particularly against autonomous driving, but he still wondered what could have happened if he had been driving that night, instead of letting the car make all the decisions.

As they entered the church there were a couple of Transcribed and flesh and blood people preparing for the next day's picnic. They had folding tables set up and they were preparing sandwiches and other edibles. Of course the Transcribed did not eat physical food, as their chassis are electrically driven. Rather they were preparing for the flesh and blood folk they were expecting. Most of them were friends and relatives of the congregants.

The picnic was more of a social mixer. The intension was to reach out to the community to show that while the Transcribed had experienced significant changes, really they were the same people they were before.

One of the Transcribed rolled up to Ralph. Her name was Sandy Wilkins and was a major contributor to the church and well regarded by the congregants. "Father, we're still waiting to get a final count of the number of people coming to the picnic. John and Martha said they were coming, but I really don't think Martha is going to make it. John was transcribed less than a year ago and Martha is still having a problem with the transition."

"Yeah, Martha is still going through the grieving process. It's hard for her. I've reached out to her a couple of times. I think she'll come around. Just give her time," said Ralph.

"There's one other man who said he might come. John Miller. He's been to a couple of services. He's not transcribed, and he worries me a little bit."

"I just think that John is trying to decide whether to be transcribed if he dies. It's a big decision. I wouldn't worry too much about it. He seems personable enough."

Christine came up to them "Hello, Sandy. Is there anything I can do to help?"

Sandy looked at Christine "We've got most of the sandwiches made. Why don't you see if they need help boxing them up?"

"Ok, I'll check it out."

Sandy looked at Ralph. "You know Father, I think Christine is becoming more and more grown up every time I see her."

"Yes, she is growing. I sometimes miss the little girl she used to be."

"The last cathedral design she did was very nice, but it seemed a little kitschy."

"It was from the Episcopal cathedral in Chicago from the late 1990's. Did you see the happy face hidden in one of the circles?"

"No, I missed that. I should have another look."

"It's on the left hand side as you face the front. It's near one of the front windows."

"I'll look for it after service tomorrow."

"If you can't find it, ask Christine. She showed it to me last week. Though I think she wants to change the design again soon, so you better look in the next couple of weeks."

"I'll be sure to ask her."

"Thanks, Sandy. I've got to go finish my sermon for tomorrow."

Ralph headed for the apartment that was at the back of the warehouse. It was the upper floor office that had been converted to a living area. The apartment was accessed by a set of stairs. Ralph's treads used what is referred to as "Gecko Treads". They had the ability to grip just about any surface as they use molecular attraction called 'van der Waals force'.

He entered his apartment. It was sparsely appointed, with a couch and a few chairs. Ralph kept them for the flesh and blood people who occasionally called. There was also a bedroom and bath facility that he maintained for Christine and a kitchen where he could cook if he so desired. But again, he only used it for the flesh and blood people who came by. Ralph still enjoyed a good meal occasionally, but he consumes it in VR. Sometimes he 'cooked' it himself, or he would enjoy it in a VR area restaurant where other Transcribed meet to mingle.

Instead of working on his sermon, he actually made a call to his lawyer, using his embedded communication facility built into his chassis. He could meet his lawyer in VR if it was appropriate. But this time it was audio only as Ralph was anxious to understand what Emily had been trying to do to their visitation arrangement with Christine.

The lawyer, Steve Macklemore, was busy, but called Ralph back after a few minutes.

"Ralph, good to talk to you again. I hope all is well, what can I do for you?"

"It's about Christine. Emily is threatening to change the visitation arrangement and also says she is going to sue for sole custody."

Ralph explained the events that happened that afternoon. Since Ralph was Transcribed, he could submit his memories as evidence, if needed.

"Ralph, truth be told, anyone can sue anyone else for anything. But there are legal requirements that have to be met in order to be successful. First off, she can bring suit to rearrange the visitation. It would be referred to Family court and if the two of you could not come to an agreement, it would be held over for the judge to decide, based on the recommendations of the family representative. They are responsible for the well-being of the children in the divorce and speak for them. While Emily probably would not be able to sue for sole custody, they might make a case for changing the dates."

"Just to prevent Christine from coming to church? I am a recognized minister of the church and she is my daughter. Don't I have the right to see that she gets a proper religious upbringing?"

"That is one of the sticky points of custody. She couldn't come right out and say that your church is less holy than hers. But she could frame the argument as part of her education. She could claim that her grades have fallen and Emily needs more time with Christine to help her learn."

"Could she get away with it?"

"It's fifty-fifty. It all depends on the recommendation from the family court adviser. Ever since the Transcribed have been given legal rights it's hard to use that as a basis for discrimination. The thing is that we don't really know what she's up to until she sends us some paperwork. So for now, just keep things as they are and don't get involved with any arguments with her. She can't do anything without the court's approval, so don't really worry about it until then."

"It sounds like this is one of those cases where only the lawyers win."

"It could be that. Cases like this could drag on for quite a while. Additionally, since this call is business related, I'll have to charge you for an hour."

"That's fine, just send me the bill."

"You know I will," joked Steve.

"I would call you a shark, but that would insult sharks," replied Ralph.

"Yeah, sharks won't bite us. Professional courtesy. I'll take a quick scan since you paid for an hour, to see if anything interesting comes up. I'll let you know if I find anything."

Ralph disconnected and looked at the group of parishioners through the window in the apartment. Christine was talking to one of the little boys that had come with his Transcribed uncle. They chattered a little bit and ran off to play outside in the back of the warehouse where there were swings and a sandbox.

His mood was rather glum as he turned to the task of composing his sermon.

CHAPTER 3

One of the issues that had to be overcome with the process of transcription was the physical layout of the replacement brain. The human brain has a wrinkled, walnut-like appearance. The purpose for the wrinkles allow for a greater number of neurons to be packed into a smaller space. If there were no folding, the human cranium would have to be larger to accommodate the larger surface area.

The physical layout of the Transcribed brain is actually upside down from the flesh and blood brain from which it is derived. As the neurons are digested, they are replicated on the underlying computer substrate in the brain box. Since the most logical way to digest the brain is from the top of the head down to the spine, the Transcribed neurons end up on the bottom, creating a bottom up brain.

It is physically supported by the computing substrate that interfaces the brain to the rest of the support equipment. The computing substrate performs a number of functions in addition to physical support. It provides for temperature regulation, coordination of signal timing, which allows for over or under clocking, and also is the vehicle which identifies and replaces neurons that no longer performs optimally.

The Transcribed brain uses microscopic quantum computers that replicate each neuron as it is identified. These neurons, however, while microscopic in size, were still larger than their evolutionary designed brothers. This results in a physically larger replacement brain. Additionally, the human brain is folded to fit inside the human cranium. There is no such constraint within the Transcribed brain and the replacement *brain is smooth. This, too, leads to a physically larger brain.*

The computer substrate is built up as the transcription proceeds. When complete, the underlying Transcribed brain ends up encased within a cube of supporting quantum computers.

So too, as the spine is Transcribed, it is spread out within its own substrate for easier access to the brain stem and spinal nerves. This allows for interfacing to external interfaces such as eyes, ears, and touch and temperature sensing. These nerves also interface to the chassis torso, arms, and head.

As a result, the physical brain-box that is the embodiment of the Transcribed brain, is a thirty centimeter cube, and attached to that is a smaller fifteen centimeter cube that provides the connection to the external chassis through a smart plug that, in itself, is a wonder. The smart plug identifies each circuit coming from the Transcribed spine and connects it to its equivalent chassis circuit. While it is referred to as a plug, it could reasonably be argued that it was a cortex in its own right.

-Life Without A Brain, The History of Transcription - 2177

On Saturday night, Emily called Ralph. Seeing that the call was from Emily, Ralph put the call on speaker.

"Ralph, I just wanted to remind you that we'll be picking up Chris about 7:00 tomorrow to take her to church with us."

Upon hearing that, Christine yelled at the phone "Mom! I don't want to go to that church! I want to stay and help Dad with his service! I'm going to be one of the acolytes tomorrow and I need to update all the stained glass for the service! If I go to your church all I do is sit around while Pastor Tim yells at us for being sinners!"

"Chris, now this is not the time to be contrary! Going to that church isn't good for you. You have friends at this church and

Pastor Tim is just trying to explain God's word to us. He's not yelling," replied Emily.

"Mom, please?" cried Christine.

"Please put your father on the phone," said Emily.

Christine handed the phone to Ralph who took it off speaker and talked privately.

"Em, do you really need to do this now? Can't it wait until next week at least? This is completely out of bounds of our agreement. We don't need to make Chris a pawn in our disagreements." Ralph said.

"Tim was very insistent. Especially after how you acted yesterday."

"Me? As I recall he was the one throwing around insults! He called me a robot!"

"You were the one who attacked him and threatened him with bodily harm!"

"Em, this is ridiculous. We can't put Christine in the middle like this. We never have. Why are you doing this now?"

"Dave has known Tim all of his life, they grew up together. Tim really wants us at the service tomorrow. There was some kind of recognition that Dave was going to receive. It was kind of last minute. It really would be nice for Chris to be there for him."

"Ok, Em, but come get her earlier. Without her helping I'll have to take more time to set up for the service."

"Ok, we'll pick her up at 6:30 then."

"Ok, she'll be ready."

Ralph turned to Christine. "Chris, your mother is very insistent that you go with them tomorrow; something about Dave getting an award at church and it would be nice for you to be there for it."

Christine took the phone and said "Mom! I won't go. I heard what the award is and it's not just for Dave it's for all the men at the church who helped do some repairs! It's not like he's the only one. I've got stuff to do here tomorrow! I'm going to be an acolyte. Daddy needs me!" Then Christine started weeping.

"I know I should have told you earlier about our decision, but we really don't want you hanging around that church. It's not good for you. Your father is really confused about what God wants."

"Mom, I really like it here! Everyone is so friendly."

"Christine, you are not old enough to make these decisions."

"Please mom!"

After a pause, Emily said "Chris, hold on. Let me speak to Dave."

Emily really didn't want to make Chris a pawn either in her disagreement with Ralph and really didn't want to see her hurt.

After a few minutes, Emily came back on the line.

"All right Chris, just this once. Dave said you were right, it's a nice thing, but all the men will be getting recognized for their service. You can stay with your father and he'll drop you off after service, but next week you start going to church with us! From now on you won't have anything more to do with that church. I'm going back to court to change the visitation arrangement. Your father will no longer have Sundays with you as long as he maintains that "church" of his. Pastor Tim will be very cross because he expected all of us to be in church. But one more week won't make a difference."

"Mom, you're not being fair."

"Christine, it's not up to you. You are too young. But you can have tomorrow to say goodbye, but from then on it will be with us. You'll get to like the people at pastor Tim's church."

"They're still boring."

"You'll come to know them better and you will learn."

Christine realized that she actually had won the argument and said, "Thank you, Mom. This really means a lot to me!" said Christine.

"You're welcome, darling. Now put your father on."

Christine handed the phone back to Ralph. And he put it back on private.

"My daughter's spiritual purity trumps your heathen church!"

"I'm not going to argue this over the phone. If you insist going forward with this, please speak to my lawyer. I'm having him draw up the papers now. We can get this sorted out without ultimatums. Let's try to keep Christine first and I'm sure we can work something out like alternating visits or something. I don't have a problem with Chris having a well-rounded upbringing. Seeing other services are good for her. Let's not make the fight about scoring points, but what is best for our daughter."

"I never could get you to see reason once you've made up your mind. I'll see you in court."

"I'll bring her by in the afternoon."

"See that you do and don't be late! We'll be going out to dinner."

"Goodbye, Em."

Ralph pressed the off key and handed the phone back to Christine.

"Ok, hon. Your mom and I agreed to let you stay for tomorrow, and I'll take you home tomorrow afternoon after the picnic. The three of you will be going out to dinner."

"What about next week?"

"I don't know, Chris, the lawyers are going to get involved now. But from what my lawyer said, your mother can't change the visitation without a court order and I doubt she can get one quickly. We'll just have to see."

"Tim's church is so hateful."

"Don't say that, hon. There are many interpretations of what God is. People have to make up their own minds."

"I really don't want to go back there."

"Don't worry about those things now. We'll get things sorted out. The one thing your mother and I agree on is how much we both love you and want the best for you. I'm sure we can come to an agreement."

"I don't want to stop coming to your church. Your folks are so nice."

"Yes, they are. But why don't you get ready for bed? We have to get ready for church in the morning, and I have a sermon to finish."

"Good night, Daddy."

"Good night, darling."

"I love you, Daddy."

Christine left to go to her bedroom and Ralph turned and faced the wall. Even though he said he had to write a sermon, he didn't type it out. He simply composed it in his mind and remembered all the salient part. It was indelibly etched in his mind.

In the morning Ralph cooked breakfast for Christine. That was the only reason that he still kept the kitchen as a kitchen in his apartment. When he entertained other flesh and blood people, he usually ordered out. But for Christine, he liked to make her breakfast especially for her.

When they finished breakfast, they went down to the church to prepare to open it for the morning's service.

Ralph turned on the lights and Christine went to unlock the door. As she opened the door, one of the other parishioners, Dale Everett was there. Ralph came rolling up to the door as Christine opened it.

"Good morning, Father!" said Dale as he came rolling up. Dale was one of the earlier Transcribed with a Segway style body and had a tendency to rock back and forth a tiny bit as he stops.

"Did you see this box here? It looks like someone left you a delivery overnight. Did you order anything?"

Ralph looked around the door at the box that Dale was pointing to. Christine stepped outside to stand behind Dale as he leaned over to examine the box.

"No, I didn't."

Christine was looking at the box as Dale reached down to pick it up. The moment he touched it, the box exploded with a terrible thunder.

The massive explosion blew the door off its hinges and pushed Ralph into the church. Dale's body was torn apart by the explosion and hundreds of pieces of metal from his body and shrapnel from the bomb flailed Christine's body.

Ralph was severely damaged by the explosion and could barely move.

Ralph attempted to call for help but his body was too damaged to make a call. His ambulatory chassis was almost completely destroyed and his connection to the net was severed. He could barely see out of what was left of the upper portion of his chassis and only because the door shielded him from the explosion, was there any part of him left conscious.

The explosion triggered the neighborhood alert and the police and fire were notified and headed for the church.

Emergency vehicles arrived in a few minutes and took stock of the situation. Dale had been killed by the explosion. It completely destroyed his computing substrate. Much of what was left of his torso was embedded in Christine. Emergency workers saw her decimated body and were certain that she would not survive.

Ralph was quickly found and emergency workers hooked a diagnostic probe to him and found that while he had significant damage to his body, his computing substrate was intact and would survive.

Through the diagnostic interface they could speak to Ralph and he could speak to them. He was in no pain as his body only registered damage as a loss of functionality, not pain, but he was paralyzed.

They told him how critical Christine's wounds were and said that they would be able to stabilize her, but her body was too badly damaged to live very long. As her parent, he had the option to have her maintained so that she could be transcribed. Christine was unconscious and was not likely to regain consciousness.

"I'm her father and I would say yes, but her mother would have to agree as well"

He gave them her number and they tried to get her on the phone.

After some minutes went by they got in touch with her and gave her the grim news.

She was devastated at the news and asked to speak to Ralph.

"The doctors are saying she's going to die."

"There's very little they can do, Em."

"I don't want to lose my baby!"

"There is another way, Emily."

"You mean turn her into a robot like you?"

"Emily, she's going to die, this is the only way to save what was the essence of our daughter."

"I'll never be able to touch her again. I'll never hold her hand. Oh God…"

"Emily, I want to save our little girl, this is the only way. But we both have to agree."

"I don't know, I just don't know. Maybe we can get her to the hospital and they can clone new organs for her."

"There isn't time. New organs take weeks to grow, but her brain will die without proper support. They can't just keep pumping oxygen into her blood; the body is too badly damaged."

"Oh God, oh god, oh god, why did this have to happen!"

"Emily we have to move her now if we're going to have any chance of saving her. It's not like my accident. We can't depend on a second miracle to save her."

"Damn you! Damn you! Goddamn you! This is all your fault! You killed my little girl!"

"Emily, please! We have to make a decision and now! Do you want to have any relationship with your daughter or do you want to let her die in peace? There is no other option."

After a pause, Emily says, "YES! DAMN YOU! DO IT! DO IT!"

Calmly, Ralph said, "Ok, I'll have her moved to the hospital. Meet us there and we can talk more. The EMTs will get me a remote so we can talk."

Surprised, Emily said, "Wait! What happened to you?"

"The bomb destroyed my chassis, my computer was slightly damaged. I can't move or speak on my own. I'm using a diagnostic connection to talk to you now."

"Are you going to be all right?"

"Yes, I'll have to get a new chassis, but I don't think I was otherwise damaged. Right now though Christine is most important. They'll get her to the hospital and I'll follow after they've taken care of her. I'll go to one of the mortgage facilities while I get a new body. I'll use a remote until it's ready and I can be mated to the new chassis."

"Was anyone else hurt?"

"Dale Everett was killed. He was closest to the bomb when it went off. He was completely destroyed. His computer was torn apart in the explosion. There is nothing to be recovered. But he shielded Christine from the worst effects of the blast. If Christine was in front of him they both would have been killed."

"I'm sorry for that. This is too much. I'll meet you at the hospital."

Ralph was put on life support through the diagnostic plug. It maintained the electrical and cooling necessary to keep him functioning while the EMTs cut away the broken and destroyed parts of his chassis.

The diagnostic plug provided basic audio and visual support but did not have arms or legs to move around. Basically the cable went from Ralph's computer to a box that allowed him to see and hear what was going on.

Through it, he could see the techs working on his body and eventually they removed the computer from the chassis, the diagnostic cable hung from it. It felt odd to be looking at his own brain.

Then they stored Ralph's brain in the emergency support frame, and moved the frame to the ambulance and headed to the medical engineering center. From there, after he was checked out, he had his brain moved to a mortgage facility for storage.

While this was going on, Christine was enveloped in medical nano-gel to preserve her body and circulate oxygen to her brain. By time Ralph was moved, Christine was gone. All that remained was the destroyed entrance to the church and the bits and pieces of Dale's destroyed chassis and computer.

While Ralph was in transit, he was in contact with the hospital and both he and Emily called in to give their permission to have Christine Transcribed. Ralph talked briefly with the transcription surgeon who was reviewing the information while he was mating with the surgical frame that would perform the transcription. The surgeon also was Transcribed.

"From what I'm seeing, your daughter was very badly injured in the explosion. I'll get more information when she arrives, but preliminarily I don't think there will be much problem transcribing her."

"I could see that her face and body was badly burned by the bomb. Did any of the shrapnel enter her brain?"

"Perhaps some small pieces may have punctured the cranium, but if that is true, there shouldn't be any brain damage. There is one issue though."

"What is that?"

"Given the extent of her injuries, it would not be advisable to make her wake up to have a conscious transcription process. I would recommend that we transcribe her while she is unconscious."

"That is how I was Transcribed. What is the problem?"

"There is a very small chance that there might be errors in her transcription because she will not be able to experience her sensorium during the process. It's not the best solution but it is the only one we have."

"What would be the problem with waking her for the transcription?"

"Several. First off, is that she would be in extreme pain if we woke her up. We can't give her any pain medications because that would interfere with the transcription process. Also, she would be extremely traumatized by the prospect of waking up on the operating table and seeing her body injured and then having to participate in the sensorium transfer that occurs as part of transcription."

"So it will be like my transcription. She'll just wake up in VR rehab in a bed."

"Yes, if you want you can be there when she wakes so her instantiation trauma could be minimized."

"Yes doctor, I would like that. I'm at the med engineering center now. I'll be mated to a remote frame and come to the hospital as soon as I can."

"Realize there is also the issue of having her memories check summed and her experiences verified before she will be given permanent legal status."

"Doctor, she's just a child, her mother and I will be able to vouch for her experiences. There can't be that many of them."

"That's true, but the process is the same, regardless of the age of the Transcribed. She'll be under a heightened review as a result."

"You mean she could die a second time."

"We don't think of it like that. If a transcription is not viable, the failed transcription is notified and immediately terminated. By legal definition that transcription was never alive in the first place. The person who failed transcription died on the operating table and their death certificate reflects that. The date and time will be the date and time of the transcription process. Not the time of the termination of the failed program.

"This is my daughter you're talking about! You're saying you're going to kill my daughter!"

"Please, Mr. Chalmers, calm down! This hospital has never had a failed transcription. And we've done hundreds of transcriptions, both conscious and unconscious. If they make it to the operating table, there is a 99% chance that they will be successfully Transcribed. But I have to inform you of all the possible outcomes. I have every confidence that she will survive the transcription."

"Ok doctor, but I am so afraid."

"I understand. It is a traumatic time for everyone. Please contact us when you get to the hospital and we'll talk further. Christine is just about ready for the operation and we'll be starting in just a few minutes."

"How long will it take?"

"I'll be examining her body and I've been reviewing the x-rays and other scans. Right now it looks like there is very little damage to her cranium so I don't think it will take too much longer than a regular transcription. Probably eight to nine hours."

"Very good doctor. I'll let you know when I roll in."

Ralph hung up and reviewed the status of his computer. His internal diagnostics showed that there was damage to his batteries and his chassis was no longer charging them. He was being maintained by the diagnostic plug.

Following his checkup and repair, he was transported to the mortgage facility. It was the facility that served as a hospital and storage for the Transcribed brains. While he was there, his computer would be in a frame in a glorified computer room. But he would be mobile through a remote. His full tactile senses and mobility would be provided by a treaded mobile platform that would give him access to the real world.

While he was mated to the remote frame, he could move around, but his range was limited to the local area where there was network support. If he went outside the area or lost contact with the engineering center, he would drop back to his frame and just have audio contact with the staff. The remote provided information about signal strength and signal delay. Also his movements would be delayed, as they had to travel wirelessly over the net to his computer. Though the delay was minor, it could affect his ability to drive or do other time sensitive operations. So in effect he was crippled. But he could get to the hospital with no problems.

Also while his remote chassis would still electronically identify him as Ralph Chalmers, he also had his name and transcription license number emblazoned on the chassis so no one would confuse him with a robot. Also, the chassis did not have a screen to display his face; only the eye stalks of his cameras and the basic assembly that gave him arms.

After about an hour the mating was complete and he made an appointment to come back in a few days to discuss the details of getting a new chassis.

Following his mating, he left the center and hailed a cab and headed to the hospital. An automated car arrived a few minutes later.

On the way, Ralph received a call.

"Ralph Chalmers?"

"Yes, who is this?"

"I'm detective Jim Moore, I'm investigating the explosion this morning. What can you tell me about it?"

"Detective, I'm on the way to the hospital. My daughter was severely injured. I really don't have time to talk right now."

"Mr. Chalmers, we need to find out what happened. It's imperative you speak to me now."

"Can you meet me at the hospital? My daughter is about to be Transcribed and I really don't want to leave her."

"Ok, I can be there in a couple of hours. I'll meet you there."

"Very well."

CHAPTER 4

Detective Jim Moore got the call just a little after 07:00 that there had been an explosion at a warehouse in the industrial district. By time he got there Ralph and Christine had been taken away. Patrolmen were still on the scene examining the remains of Dale Everett and the results of the blast.

Locating the responding patrolman, Jim asked what occurred.

Reading the officers name badge, the detective said, "Officer Hays, can you tell me what occurred and what this place is? It doesn't look like a warehouse."

"It's not. This is the temple for the Church of the Transcribed."

"Hardly looks like a church. You mean the robots go here to pray?"

"Yeah, I guess. I don't see anything inside that you would find in a church, though. Even for robots."

Examining the scene from the front of the church, Jim saw that the doors to the space had been blown in. There were scorch marks on the walls and sidewalk where the detonation occurred. The banister to the doors was a tangle of metal. In the middle of the stoop just in front of the door, there was a bare spot devoid of any scorching.

"It's pretty obvious where the blast happened. Is there anything left of the bomb?"

"The bottom of the box it came in is embedded in the concrete from the power of the explosion. Not much else appears to be here. There is shrapnel everywhere. Parts of it could be from the bomb, and parts could be from the robot that was standing in front of the box when it detonated. It tore him apart pretty well. Just the lower part of his chassis is left and there are multiple holes in the box from where the overpressure and other shrapnel pieces pierced it. It was the heat and the overpressure that opened up his brain box and shorted his power cells. At least that is what the tech thinks."

"So he was the first one on the scene, huh?" Meaning that he was at ground zero for the explosion.

"He and a flesh and blood kid, a girl, and another robot that was blown into the warehouse when he was hit with one of the doors."

"A kid?" the detective is repulsed that someone would do this horrible thing to a child.

"What was the girl doing here?"

"She was the daughter of the minister of the church."

"She was the robot's daughter?"

"That's what the EMT techs said."

"Did she live?"

"Depends. She was pretty well chewed up by the pieces of the bomb and the other robot. The techs said her body wouldn't last too long. The parents are probably going to have her Transcribed, too."

"Another robot. Why would any parent do that to their kid?" The term robot is considered pejorative among the Transcribed, but many in society use the term as an epithet or when referring to the Transcribed when they were not in earshot.

"Who knows, you'd think they'd just let her die in peace."

Walking up to the remains of Dale Everett, he looked at the scorched chassis and pieces of Dale's torso all over the ground. He peered into some of the blast holes. Taking a small flashlight from his pocket he shined the light into the box.

"Not much left in here. Was there much of a fire?"

"Not really, there really wasn't anything to burn to speak of. The firemen sprayed it all down with retardant when they got here but there weren't any other flames after the blast."

"Anyone know who sent the call?"

"Not sure, we think he did," pointing to the chassis of Dale.

"How could he do that?"

"Not sure, we also got the alert from the explosion sensors so it could have been either."

Stepping into the darkened space, with the patrolman following, he saw where the doors ended up. Inside the warehouse/temple one door had been blown deep into the space and careened off the back wall. Another door was turned over and there were obvious skid marks and the remains of another chassis in the middle of the space.

"This is where the other robot ended up. As near as we can tell he was behind one of the doors when the bomb went off and was blown here. The door protected him from the overpressure and heat, but the force of the door hitting him destroyed his chassis."

"Looks like they had to saw him out of the box. Is that what happened?"

"Yes, the emergency engineering guys hooked him up to a plug after they got here. Then after they got him stabilized they went at this box with saws. The sent the brain to the mortgage warehouse for housing. They said something about him getting a remote so he can walk around until he gets a new chassis."

"This guy lived?"

"Yeah."

"He have a name?"

"Ralph Chalmers. He owns this place. It's his church."

Looking at the almost completely empty space the detective said, "This is a church?"

"That's what they told me."

"Doesn't look like much of a church."

"What do I know? I'm not a robot."

"Any word on what the bomb was?"

"Not too much to go on, really. The sniffers say Semtex. It was probably pretty crude, but stuffed with it. Also it looks like it was packed with scrap metal and ball bearings for shrapnel."

"How big was the box?"

"We can't tell the exact size but the bottom of the bomb was the box it came in. And that was about a meter by a meter and a half. It may have been about 25 centimeters high."

"How do you know it was a crude bomb?"

"The blast was almost completely spherical. There was nothing in the box to direct the force of the bomb in one direction or another. If they wanted to do the maximum damage to the building, they would have put a plate on one side of the box to force the overpressure against the door. They just put a shit load of explosives in it and hoped for the best."

"Not too bright. How about triggering, any idea what triggered it?"

"Nothing there yet either. From what the one robot who survived said, it may have been proximity or remote detonation."

"Why do you say that?"

"Apparently the guy who got fried was standing next to it waiting for the door to open and when they did, the kid came out and he was bending over the box about to pick it up when it went off. So it was set to blow when anyone touched it or remote and someone triggered it while they were watching."

"Do you really think some fuck would really blow up a kid?"

"There are some real assholes around."

"Since it's a bomb, it's definitely a hate crime, but who?"

"Someone who doesn't like robots, I guess."

"That narrows it down about half of the city."

"Yeah, no real clues in that."

"Give me this guy's contact information. I guess I have to go to the mortgage warehouse to talk to him."

"If he gets a remote, that means he can move around, just

not too far. He said he would be going to the hospital to check on his kid once he got hooked up."

"I'll call him and see if I can't track him down. What about forensics, are they coming?"

"Yeah, they're on their way here now."

"I want to find out about the triggering of the bomb and where it came from. Did the sniffer analysis say anything more about the explosive?"

"The tracer chemicals in the explosion show that it was made in the last two years and it came from a manufacturer in this country."

"Anything more detailed?"

"Not right now. The forensics people will get a more detailed analysis when they take detailed swaps from the debris. They'll have the manufacturer and exact date and batch numbers from that."

"This industrial park is pretty deserted; no residential spaces here. Did the 'temple' here have security cameras?"

"Not that we can tell, but some of the other buildings did."

"I'll need to see those videos. Send them to me when you get them."

"Ok."

"Has anyone else shown up?"

"Apparently they were opening up to have service so there are some parishioners being interviewed by the other patrolmen who are here."

"Where are they now?"

"Around the other side of the building giving interviews. We didn't want them here while we did our work."

"Good thinking. Did anyone have anything useful to say?"

"Not really. 'How could they do this?' 'He was a nice man.' 'That poor girl.' That stuff."

"Ok, get those interviews to me, too, when you get them. How many have shown up?"

"About fifteen to twenty."

"All robots?"

"Yeah."

"Doesn't seem like a big congregation for such a large space."

"Maybe they expect to grow."

"Might be a reason to bomb the place, you never know. You know how folks get about Transcribed's being the same as people."

"Yeah, you hear a lot of folks badmouthing the robots, and tipping and stuff, but this is the first time I've heard of anyone bombing them."

CHAPTER 5

*B*rain transcription, while simple in concept, is anything but. Once the cranium has been opened, a grey mat of nano-devices, each smaller than a neuron, spread on the surface of the brain. The process is pre-programmed into the devices and the surgeon simply oversees. When the entire surface has been covered, the nano-mat starts to probe each cell. The nucleus, axon, and dendrites are probed for functionality. Where a dendrite and axon meet, there is a gap called a synapse. The gap is jumped by neurotransmitters from the axon to the dendrite. The nano-probe examines these synapses for functionality. The way a synapse responds to stimulation is examined. Once this examination is performed, the probes then insert themselves at each synapse, and a microscopic quantum computer is added to the computing substrate at the other end of the probe, replicating and mimicking the action of the neuron. Once this mimicry is performed, the cell is excised and discarded. The probes connect to a single quantum neuron computer that exactly replicates the function of the replaced neuron. However, the probes do not release neurotransmitter molecules to cross the synaptic gap. Instead a micro-volt of electricity is released from the replicated axon to the dendrite of the next cell. This electrical stimulation replicates the effect of the neurotransmitter molecule.

The discarded cell is put in the medical waste receptacle. Effectively turning the flesh and blood brain to mush. The blood supply to the neurons is blocked off by other parts of the nano-mat so the patient's body doesn't die from blood loss.

Once this is performed, the next cell is examined, probed,

mimicked, and replicated by another quantum computer neuron. Synapse, by synapse, neuron, by neuron, each cell in the brain is replaced by millions of quantum micro-computers.

If this is all there was to the process, it would go in a very straightforward manner. Simply replace every neuron with a quantum computer and voila, a Transcribed brain.

However, it becomes a bit more difficult to interface this collection of quantum computers to the outside world. We see, but not the way a camera sees. We hear but not the way a microphone listens. The optic nerve and visual cortex is one of the most complex sub-processors of the human brain and work in concert to allow the brain to make sense out of the world that it sees. Fully ninety percent of the information presented to the brain is through the optic nerves. Most of the understanding of what the brain comprehends results in a visual reference. People can recall quite vividly events they see through their eyes. But can rarely recall the smells (though that is a complex mechanism as well). And while the experience of pain is immediate, thankfully, no one can re-experience pain, only the memory of pain.

As the nano-mat works through the visual cortex, it must also ingest the optic nerves and the retina. The retina is a mat of neurons that respond to a range of photons in a very small spectrum of energy. The colors and patterns create reactions within the optic nerve, which is processed by the visual cortex. This reaction is presented to the brain as a visual memory. So the optic nerve can see the color green and shapes of branches and the visual cortex matches the patterns and colors to remembered images and presents the brain with an interpretation of a tree. It is a spectacularly complex process and must be replicated accurately within the computer substrate of the Transcribed's brain.

To interface the outside world to the Transcribed's brain through visual imagery, an electronic device that is sensitive to the visual spectrum is interfaced to the replicated optic nerves. So, too, the neurons that controlled the muscles that moved and focused the cornea are also replicated. So the brain triggers nerves that move muscles that move the eyeball. Movements of micro motors attached to the device replicate this action. To simply call this a camera is undermining its incredible complexity.

Also the world of VR is created within a computer by directly stimulating the replaced retina with the imagery of the VR world being presented. This, again, is an over-simplification of the actual process. This can only be accomplished by the incredibly rapid computation available to quantum-based computers.

Hearing, also, is a complex replication process that requires the ingesting of the cochlea and cochlear nerves. Without this process, audio information cannot be interfaced to the Transcribed's brain.

Smell, however, is unique for the brain. It is the only sense the brain has where the neurons that are triggered by the macro-molecules of scent directly trigger a response in the brain, without being pre-processed by a cortical component. The olfactory bulb directly stimulates the hypothalamus and amygdala. These directly stimulate memories and responses in the brain. Taste through the tongue is similarly directly attached through the brain stem to the hypothalamus and works in concert with the olfactory nerves to produce coordinated responses to pleasant and unpleasant tastes and smells.

Movement and sensation also were less than straightforward in transcription. Much of the reactive movements of the body are contained within the brain stem and lower structures of the spinal cord. So the involuntary movement caused when someone touches something hot, is not reacted on by the brain, but done semi-autonomously by the muscles and neurons in the spine. So ingestion of the spinal cord down to at least the 12 vertebrae must be performed. Otherwise the act of movement could not be coordinated with either the flesh and blood brain or the one made out of silicon neurons.

Even the act of balancing and walking is not so much directly driven by the brain, but is a coordinated effort of the semi-circular canals (which are also ingested and replicated) which give the body a sense of location in three dimensional space, the brain stem and the visual cortex and overseen by the upper cogitative functions. Calling it a balancing act is truly well deserved. And the act of walking upright is a process of controlled falling where synchronized movement of the legs and feet, catch the body in a deliberate fall when it moves its torso off center. This synchronization is a learned process as any toddler can tell you.

The end result is that the process of transcription is more than just eating away the neurons and of trading them in for grains of silicon. All of this interfacing and coordination is overseen by the computer substrate that performs the coordination and timing of signals. It also is considered to be the operating system of the Transcribed brain.

Several companies had invested hundreds of billions of dollars of research in creation of the quantum micro-computers and associated operating systems that interface with the substrate. The manufacturers initially created unique families of computers that only interfaced with the substrate of the manufacturers. However, federal regulation intervened and all manufacturers of the neurons and substrate had to adhere to an industry standard of interfaces and signals so that transcriptions could be effectively done without corporate lock-in.

Transcribeware, and BrainTran, were the two leaders of the industry. While the interfaces were compatible, reaction time, number of inputs/output, and specialty type neurons were constantly being developed for the after-market upgrade crowd. The sense of taste, for example, could be enhanced to be more sensitive to chemical diagnosis. Thus the Transcribed's tongue could be turned into a chemical lab. This is paired with a library of known "tastes" that can be detected by the upgraded tongue.

Likewise, the sense of hearing can be augmented as well, but is tempered by the processing abilities of the audio cortex to integrate into the overall sensorium. So while it is possible to interface to an electronic device that can hear from DC to the multi-kilohertz range of sounds, there are only so many cochlear nerves. So hearing can be offset to hear higher frequencies, the ability to "hear" in the normal frequencies is lost.

Vision is also limited by the ability of the visual cortex. So while cameras could see from infrared to x-ray frequencies of light energy, this ability can only be understood if it is offset to the visual cortex's range. So too, the ability to see out of more than two eyes so the Transcribed could have a visual sense of three hundred and sixty degrees is not possible with the visual cortex that has been the result of millions of years of evolution.

But, what was gained by the transcription of flesh and blood to silicon was, by some, to be viewed as a positive, if not a boon. Neurons age and change and die, and are not easily replaced by the brain. This is not true of the silicon variety. When they perform below what is considered nominal, they are replaced automatically by the computer substrate.

This means that the Transcribed brain is much more durable than the flesh and blood brain. The lifespan of the Transcribed is indefinite. Some would say immortal, but that implies overcoming the heat death of the universe and that is a much bigger question. But, as long as the substrate has *power and can provide replacements, the brain, and thus the entity of the mind, can continue living.*

It would seem that in all this transcription process, the idea of an immaterial "soul" is abandoned. And for many, it is. Though, too, those that were religious or spiritual prior to being Transcribed, claim not to have lost their spiritual nature as a result of being turned into talking sand.

It is a matter of some conjecture whether this means that somewhere in all that quanta there is a connection to "God" however It is perceived, or the fidelity of the transcription is so great that faith of the Transcribed are recreated in total in the Transcribed brain.

-Life Without A Brain, The History of Transcription - 2177

When he arrived at the hospital, Ralph identified himself to the hospital AI and he was directed to the operating waiting room.

When he got to the waiting room, Emily and David were already there, and also Pastor Tim. He was consoling the couple and saying prayers as he read from the Bible.

Ralph took one look at the pastor and was surprised at the level of anger he felt. Since he had been transcribed, he had much more control of his emotions and could simply adjust the settings on his integrated control systems. Normally, he let them auto adjust so that he could experience the world in as normal a way as possible. Ralph adjusted his anger down, because he knew that it wouldn't help the situation with Christine.

Tim was not so charitable and when he saw Ralph's remote he turned to him furiously.

"What is that robot doing here? It was responsible for kidnapping your daughter and exposing her to the blast. It probably directed your child to check the box first so it could protect its cowardly frame."

"I'm Christine's father and I have more right to be here than you! You have done nothing but cause confrontation from the first moment we met. If you don't leave right now, I'll call security and I'll have you thrown out!"

"I am a duly registered pastor and I am allowed to be here to provide pastoral care to my flock. You're nothing more than a drink dispenser. Ralph Chalmers' wife became a widow eight years ago. You are not him. At very best you are a low level simulacrum and a poor one at that. You're just a talking computer. You deserve no rights, least of all to be called human."

Emily shouted, "Stop it both of you! I can't stand it anymore. I've lost my husband and now I've lost my daughter. All I can do from now on is look at a talking picture of her. I don't know if I can take that." Looking at Ralph, she said, "Tim has been saying that we should stop the transcription. She died in the explosion. We should let her go."

"Emily, no!" said Ralph.

"Trust me, Emily," said Tim. "It's better this way. She is in the hands of God now. Her soul is gone. There is nothing more you can do for her. Stop this abomination. Her body will be defiled. Let us take her now and bury her with all the dignity a human being deserves."

David had his arms around Emily's shoulder comforting her. "Tim is right. Christine is gone; let her go. This is cruel to you and her memory. I've known Tim all my life he is a kind man, a loving man. He doesn't want to see you be constantly hurt by having a vacuum cleaner with Christine's voice."

Tim said, "Remember if you go through with this, you will be committing a sin! You can never bring that thing to church. God will be furious with you. You both could be excommunicated."

Emily stood up, her face grim, and turned to Tim furiously, "How DARE you! How dare you talk to me like that! You can't put this on me! This is not the time to talk to me about God! My daughter is still alive! And you want me to finish killing her? I can't do that! I can't be responsible for another death! Get out! GET OUT!"

Tim looked at her. "I'll go, of course. But you must not allow this defilement to go on. Please come to reason and stop this terrible thing."

"Get out!" she yells.

Tim stormed toward the door and turned to David, "David you must speak sense to her. If you allow this to go on you'll put yourself on the wrong side of the church. Surely you can see that this is an abomination!"

Dave stood and looked at Emily, "Em, I love you. I'll stay with you and support any decision you make." He looks at Tim and said, "You've made me have to choose between my family and wife, and the church. Tim, I've known you since I was a kid, but you've gone too far. You can't ask this."

"God will judge you both! You've made him very angry! He'll throw Christine's soul in hell because of what you've done!"

Ralph turned to Tim, "All right, that's enough, get the hell out now! I'm calling security."

Ralph then electronically contacted the hospital AI and informed it of a disturbance in the waiting room. The AI announced over the intercom, "Attention, Reverend Tim Misinger, this is a formal instruction to vacate. Security will arrive in less than thirty seconds. You may leave on your own now or you will be formally charged with trespassing and arrested. Your credentials as a registered pastoral care representative will be reviewed for cancellation."

Tim stormed out the door.

"Thank you, David," said Ralph.

"This isn't for you! I hadn't thought about the Transcribed much before Emily and I started dating. I've been going to Tim's church for as long as I can remember and I've never seen him like this. I love Emily and she is more important to me than Tim's insane beliefs."

Emily turned to Ralph, "I still don't know if this is the right thing or not. But I can't do it. I can't pull the plug on my daughter while there is a hope, any hope that she'll be all right."

"I understand, Em. It'll be all right. I'll be with her and you can see her as soon as she's been through rehab."

"I'll never hold her, really hold her. The most I'll ever do again is to visit her in some make believe fairy land."

"I understand, Em. It will be all right. Have you had a chance to ask how she is doing? I talked to the doctor before I left the mortgage center, but I haven't heard anything since then."

"No, we've been talking to Tim the whole time."

"How did he find out?"

"We had just walked into church and Tim greeted us at the door. He had just asked us where Christine was when I got the call. David was telling him how we were allowing you one more day with Christine. It seemed like he knew something was up when he saw my face. He started smiling when I heard that there was a bomb. But as he listened to my side of the conversation he knew that something was wrong."

"After we got off the phone I told him that Christine had been hurt and that we had to go to the hospital," said David.

"He offered to come with us to provide care. We told him that he shouldn't leave his flock, but he was insistent. He said that he would have one of the other ministers perform the service. This was a terrible crisis for us and he should be with us until Christine was out of danger."

Ralph said, "That's very odd, him smiling like that. Let me go check on Chris. They were about to start the operation when I came in."

Both David and Emily knew that Ralph would be able to interface with the Hospital AI directly and get a direct line to the surgeon if necessary. Ralph rode over to the couple and stopped. Ralph then called the Hospital AI.

"This is Father Ralph Chalmers. I'm Christine Chalmers father. What is the status of my daughter's transcription?" Ralph also was a registered pastoral care representative, but he had rarely been called to provide care.

After a few seconds later another person came on the line, "I'm Walter Franks, the doctor's nurse, how can I help you?"

"I'm Christine's father, how is the operation going?"

"The doctor is overseeing the procedure directly, we've just started. From the first examinations, she should have a successful transcription. There are significant injuries to her internal organs, but they can provide support along with our surgical gear long enough to complete the transcription. Her cranium is intact, her spine, and major peripheral nerves have only minor damage, so we don't foresee any serious problems."

"Thank you. Do you have any idea how long it will take?"

"Probably another five or six hours at minimum. Since she'll have an unconscious transcription so we're going to be taking it extra slow so there shouldn't be any transcription errors. Her brain is showing signs of activity commensurate with the severe injuries that she has maintained. Again these are things that we've seen before and don't expect any surprises."

"Thank you again. I'm still very anxious, as you can imagine."

"I understand. In my transcription I was conscious, and I was terrified through the whole thing. I sometimes think it's better this way."

"In Christine's case, I think it's for the better. She's had enough trauma."

"Yes. I have to return to the doctor now. You can follow the progress by addressing our site and the hospital AI will give you any updates as we get them."

"OK, we'll talk later."

Ralph wondered what possible purpose a nurse would be in the case of a transcription. Even the doctor had very little actual work to do. The process of transcription is done entirely through an active nano-machine mat that was placed on the open cranium. The nano machines examined each neuron, dendrite and synapse and examined the way it operated on many different levels. It inserted microscopic probes at each synaptic gap and replaced the operation of the cell with an identical one in the computing substrate. Once it was verified that the cell operated as well as the one replaced, it removed the original and discarded it. The brain eventually was completely eaten by the process.

Throughout the process the doctor was more of a project manager than someone who wielded a scalpel. Ralph had no idea how the nurse would assist in a process like that once the cranium was exposed.

Ralph turned to Emily and gave them the update.

Now that he had to sit through the process that he himself once went through, he could understand Emily's anxiety.

"Em, this is not what I wanted, please know this. I know how hard this is for you, but really you aren't alone. Christine will return to us. She will have a wonderful and full life. You'll see her again today."

"I know, Ralph, but it's so hard. I had to go through this with you and now with her. It's like everything is being stolen from me. Everything that I ever loved is being so changed. And you can't say that this won't change her. No matter how she comes out of the surgery. No matter how lifelike we make her new body, she won't be the same little girl I gave birth to."

"Em, please."

"No really, she'll think faster, she'll be able to know anything, she won't have to go to school. Why should she when she can download everything from the net? And she'll have complete control over her emotions and can just dial them to whatever setting she likes.

"And she'll never know the joys of motherhood. She'll never give birth. Any boy that she would be interested in has to be Transcribed too. She'll be so lonely."

"I can't say that you're wrong, Em, but this was forced on us. I never asked to be Transcribed. I didn't want our daughter to have this burden. But we had no choice. We would have lost our little girl."

As they anxiously awaited further news about Christine, a man walked, in, wearing a badge on his lapel.

He looked at Ralph's mobile remote he said, "Are you Ralph Chalmers?"

Ralph turned to him, "Yes, are you the detective I spoke with?"

"Is this about what happened to Christine?" asked Emily.

"Yes, Em. He called me when I was on my way to the hospital"

He turned to look at Emily and Dave, he asked, "Did you see what happened?"

"No. I'm Emily's mother and this is my husband, Dave."

"Is there someplace we can talk, Mr. Chalmers?"

"Actually, it's Father Chalmers. I'm sure we can find an office or someplace to talk. Let me ask the Hospital."

Ralph conferred with the AI (who was actually an SAI) and was directed to an office down the hallway.

The AI unlocked the door as they approached. Ralph and the detective entered and the detective closed the door and sat at the desk. Ralph moved the other chairs and positioned himself in front of the desk, and faced the detective.

The detective looked up at the ceiling, a pointless gesture really, since the AI had several cameras in each room, "I am Detective James Moore, and I am conducting official police business. Please stop all recording and monitoring until we leave this office."

The SAI replied, "Detective Moore, you have been credentialed and recording is now suspended."

The detective turned to Ralph and took a micro recorder out of his pocket and placed it on the desk in front of him. It would record visual and audio information in three hundred and sixty degrees. "As I stated before, I am Detective James Moore and I am conducting an investigation into the event that occurred this morning. I am speaking to Father Ralph Chalmers. I'm sorry to have to do this at such a traumatic time, but it is essential to get as many facts as we can so we can get a good idea what happened. Do you prefer being called Father?"

"Just Ralph is fine."

"Very good, can you tell me what happened this morning?"

"My daughter and I were just getting ready to open the church. She had opened the door and Dale was waiting for us."

"Then what happened?"

"I was standing behind the right side door, and Christine had opened the left door and stepped outside. Dale was standing in the doorway waiting for us to open. Dale had noticed the package when he rolled up. He said something about seeing it there when he arrived. I was leaning around the door when Dale moved to pick up the package. That's when the explosion occurred."

"So you were behind the door where the package was found?"

"Yes, they're steel doors and it protected me from the worst of the blast. We had intentions of replacing them with glass doors when we did our renovations, since the building used to be a warehouse and we wanted to improve its appearance."

"Did you see what triggered the blast? Did any of you touch the package before it exploded?"

"No, no one touched it. Dale was reaching for it and Christine was behind Dale."

"What happened when the package exploded?"

"The blast blew the door into me. When it hit me, it severed my upper body and pushed me into the church. There's nothing in the space to speak of, we don't need pews or anything else. The explosion tumbled me over and I rolled over several times and bounced off the far wall. I don't have much after that. My internal diagnostics were going crazy and I couldn't see much. I think I still had something connected, since I could see, but it was intermittent and wasn't pointed at the door. I was paralyzed. I couldn't move my treads or any part of my body."

"Did you see what happened to Dale and your daughter?"

"Yes, I'll have those images for the rest of my life. When the explosion happened, my chassis went into automatic over clocking, meaning I experienced everything in slow motion. As the door pushed against me I could see Dale coming apart and the pieces of him hit Christine. The heat from the blast hit her face and upper body. I saw her flesh burn... I... don't remember much else."

"Thank you, Father. We'll need a copy of your memories, visual, audio, and any diagnostic information you have. It will help us catch who did this."

"Do you have any information?"

"Nothing yet, we're still examining the scene. It looks like a crude bomb, possibly detonated remotely, not on a timer."

"That means that whoever did this was watching as this happened? They saw my daughter in front of the bomb!"

"Ralph, please don't jump to conclusions. We don't have all the facts yet. It could have been a sensor trigger, too, and they can be pretty tricky. We're still examining the pieces."

"And Dale, what did you do with Dale?"

"We contacted his next of kin, his sister. She is coming to retrieve him."

"Poor Dale. He was one of our first full time parishioners. He made some suggestions on how we conduct our service. He came to every service. He was so very dedicated."

"Unfortunately, his chassis and computer were completely destroyed. There was nothing we could retrieve from his memories. But at least he didn't suffer."

Ralph looked up at the man, "Detective, obviously, you are not Transcribed. When the explosion happened, Dale went into automatic over clocking. I can say that Dale felt every microsecond of the explosion. He was conscious during every part of it. He could probably see the damage that he was doing to Christine, and could do nothing to stop it. He was one of the kindest, gentlest souls I have ever known. He didn't deserve that. He suffered, I know he suffered."

"I'm sorry, I didn't know."

"It's all right. He was probably the one who called in the explosion. I know I tried as I was being blown across the room. But by that time I didn't have any connection to the net."

"I don't have that information yet."

"We'll want to have a service for Dale. Did his sister say when she would be arriving?"

"She's coming in from Seattle. She'll be here this afternoon."

"Can you have her contact me when she arrives? I'd like to talk to her."

"I'll pass the information along. One last question, do you have any idea who might have done this?"

"No, not really. We've been reviled by many groups, but no one ever did anything physical before."

"Do you have that information available?"

"It's in the church archives. I'll have someone get it to you."

"Thank you, Father. We'll probably talk again. I'm sure there are going to be more questions as this unfolds."

"Yes, of course. Now, if you don't mind, I'd like to go back to the waiting room. It's too early to expect any news, but I need to be there for Emily."

"How did Emily find out?"

"I called her after I was connected by emergency support. She was just getting to church."

"And David is her husband?"

"Yes, they've been married a few years."

"Ok, Father, we'll be in touch."

"Thank you."

They left the room and returned to the waiting area. The detective asked to speak to Emily and David and they left. Ralph presumed that they'll get the same interview that he had just received. They returned a short time later.

The detective returned to his office and received the preliminary report about the bomb. They acquired the shrapnel that was removed from Christine's body and the parts and components that blew through Dale's chassis. From the information they could gather, the bomb was a crude device that had been wired to a contact trigger at the top of the box. They suspect that it was supposed to go off when it was opened. But either the switch triggered early or fell off and triggered.

It contained bricks of Semtex packed with lead pellets and pieces of metal. It was designed, supposedly to penetrate the chassis of Transcribed and kill the computer inside. It worked on Dale, but also killed the body of Christine. From the pieces they got from the hospital, most of the damage to Christine came from the pieces that flew off Dale as he was blown apart. This was a hateful bomb, designed to kill not frighten. The point of terror is to cause fright in the living.

The box itself was a standard plastic shipping crate. From the statement and memories of Ralph, he did not see the shipping label as he was behind the door when the bomb went off. But Ralph said Dale implied that it had a standard shipping label on it.

The box could have come from anywhere and it would have been simple to affix a counterfeit label on it. Examination of the blast scene did not have any more clues than what was already known.

The interview of the congregants didn't have any relevant information, though examination of the church's archive of hateful emails, videos, and other messages were still being examined.

From the review of security cameras in the area, the box was put in place about three o'clock in the morning. A hooded figure was seen putting it next to the door and running off. Tracking him back through various cameras showed him losing himself in the street crowd nearby. The figure appeared male in stature but that was the only thing that could be determined. He seemed to appear out of nowhere from a side alley carrying the box.

The only thing that stood out, at least initially, was that the church that Dave, Emily, and Christine attended appeared to be virulently anti-Transcribed. Regularly referring to the Transcribed as robots, "unliving machines" that talked like the departed. Jim had no real antipathy toward the Transcribed. The law said that a properly Transcribed person who had been properly licensed was a human and had to be treated as such. He often referred to them as robots without thinking of the pejorative nature of the term. But this First Baptist Church felt that it was their duty to say that the Word of God did not extend to anything except flesh and blood people.

He had interviewed Ralph, David, and Emily and their stories were substantially similar. The pastor of the Church, one Tim Misinger, seemed to react about the bomb *before* he had been told about it.

Emily had received the call from Ralph just as they were about to enter the church and from the frantic nature of Emily's call, he appeared to be pleased by the information, before Emily said anything. He was appropriately horrified to learn the girl had been killed. He also brought significant pressure on the family to not have the girl Transcribed. The mother and father agreed to the transcription as the only recourse to save anything about her. The pastor was furious and had threatened to excommunicate them from the church.

He would follow up with Pastor Tim.

Ralph, Emily, and Dave were still waiting to hear news about Christine's transcription. It had been hours since it was started. The hospital AI was of little assistance saying that it wasn't a process that could be given a progress meter. Major components of Christine's brain had been successfully Transcribed and were being integrated into the supporting computer substrate that would form the basis of the operating structure that formed the computer substrate.

A number of the congregation, after being interviewed by the police, went to the hospital to help and provide comfort to the family.

Ralph greeted them with joy and was touched by the out-pouring of sympathy and support. Emily and Dave, on the other hand were overwhelmed by all the Transcribed coming into the waiting room. It directly touched on the reasons that they were there in the first place. Emily burst into tears and ran from the room followed by David.

Sandy Gibbons, one of the congregants, said, "Father, this is terrifying! Why did this happen? Why do they hate us so much?"

"Sandy, I don't know. I've never seen this level of hatred in my life. I am devastated. I really don't know what to do now. I feel I should leave. I don't know if I can go on. I never wanted anyone to get hurt. And while I grieve for my daughter, I can't forget what was done to Dale. He helped to set up the church. He had taken seminary in his younger years but went on to become an architect, as you know. He helped design the church that we use in VR. I can't, I just can't have this happen to anyone else."

"Father, you must go on. We need you. You are our driving force! Through you we see God!"

"I can't do this. One of the ministers can take over. I haven't had time to think. All this is just overwhelming."

"Father, please, take time to think, of course. The congregation and I will support you in anything you want to do. Also, know that on the way over the others of the congregation and myself decided to set up a trust fund for Christine. We will make sure that the material issues right now are taken care of. Bob is downstairs right now working with the hospital AI making arrangements. Her stay in VR, her transcription, and her chassis down payment will be completely paid for."

Ralph collapsed both internally and externally. His torso doubled over and his arms covered his face/screen. The rhythmic movement of his torso mirrored his sobbing.

After some minutes, Ralph stood up.

"The words 'Thank you' are completely inadequate to the words I want to say. I am literally speechless. Thank you."

The parishioners stayed with Ralph for a time but soon sensed that he wanted to be alone. They made their goodbyes and left a short time later. After the others had left, Dave and Emily returned to the waiting room.

Progress reports from the surgical suite and the hospital AI were regular and uplifting, as they said that the procedure was going fine. However the time seemed to drag for the three of them.

The three of them were there for about another hour when a person from the hospital came in.

"Mister and Mrs. Chalmers? My name is Susan Tellers. I'm from the hospital Social Services department." She looked at Dave and Emily, and she incorrectly assumed David and Emily were Christine's parents.

David looked at her and said, "I'm her step father, David. Her father is over there," he said, pointing at Ralph.

"Excuse me, I'm so sorry," she said. Ralph rolled up to her.

"Would you please come with me?" whereupon she guided them out of the waiting room to a nearby office.

Susan sat behind a desk with a tablet in her hand.

"Mr. And Mrs. Chalmers, I am so sorry for your loss. I understand that the procedure is going well. But still this must be such a traumatic time for you both."

"Yes," said Emily.

"I know this must be terrible for you, but we have to deal with certain issues. It is the matter of your daughter's remains."

"You mean her body?"

"Yes, there are some that want to have a ceremony."

"We just disposed of mine as medical waste, but this is different."

"I don't know if I can handle this. It's too soon."

"But Em, our daughter lives. She's alive now. You'll see her today. This doesn't have to be taken care of right now. Whatever we do, Chris might want to be a part of it."

"I just can't deal with this. No, I just don't know what to do. I don't think Tim would allow us a funeral."

"But it shouldn't be a funeral, it should be a celebration. Let's just leave it for now. We can talk about it later."

"Mr. and Mrs. Chalmers, we can hold the remains for a few days, but it is something you'll have to decide on. We can recommend a number of services that would be appropriate for your daughter and theology, if you so choose."

"Can we see her?" asked Emily.

"You mean view the remains?"

"Yes, I want to say goodbye to her."

Tellers was initially confused as Christine would soon be alive in VR rehab.

"We won't deny you, of course, but it really isn't recommended. As Christine is still alive, there is no need to identify the remains."

"But she's my daughter," said Emily, almost in a whisper.

Tellers attempted to put it as delicately as possible, "As I said, it isn't recommended. The transcription process is quite harsh and leaves the body difficult to view. Additionally there were the effects of the explosion."

Emily started to weep. Ralph felt that he should comfort her somehow, but felt uncomfortable putting his metal arm on her shoulders. He looked up at the woman and said, "Thank you. We'll have to have a discussion about this. We'll get back to you."

"Of course. You can reach me through the hospital AI." The woman then left and closed the door behind her.

Emily's weeping subsided and she lifted her tear-streaked head to Ralph. "Oh, God, why did this have to happen to our little girl, Ralph? She didn't deserve this. This is all your fault! You killed our little girl!"

"Emily, please…"

"No, dammit! You had to go and start this whole God-thing of yours! Your self-righteousness destroyed our marriage! You had to separate yourself from us! You and that damn religion of yours! YOU BASTARD!"

Ralph dialed down his emotions to keep from responding angrily. He knew that Emily was overwrought with emotions. He would have been too if he had left his emotions on auto.

"Emily," Ralph pleaded, "our daughter is alive. All that she was, all that she is will be saved! She has been terribly hurt, but she will survive."

"Where? In a goddamn box? How am I supposed to love a box of metal and wires? How is that ever the same? And I can't live in FIVR with her! It's not the same, and you know it!"

"Emily, she's my daughter, too! I never wanted this to happen to her or anyone!"

She shook her head and said, "Maybe Tim was right. Maybe I should have just let her pass. Maybe we should just bury her. She's gone, and I can never bring her back. This isn't a fitting end to her life."

"Emily, no, please, you can't mean that."

"I think I do. If we don't both agree to the transcription, they'll have to stop. My daughter is dead and this is just defilement."

"Emily, I'm pleading with you, don't do this!"

"Go get Dave. I want to talk to him."

"Ok, I'll go get him." Terrified, Ralph left the office and returned to the waiting room.

"Dave, would you come with me, please?"

"Sure, Ralph, what's going on?"

"It's Emily. She wants to stop the transcription."

"What?"

They headed out of the waiting room and went down the hall to the office.

As they went, Ralph said, "She's starting to think that Tim was right and that she should let Chris pass. And if we both don't agree they'll have to stop the procedure."

Dave said, "She's really hurt right now. She's not thinking rationally."

"I think that's true too. Maybe you can help her sort out her feelings. I don't think she has a whole lot of faith in me right now."

When they entered the office, Emily was still weeping in the chair. She looked up and saw Dave, and got up and ran to him and hugged him.

"Oh Dave, please help," she sobbed. Emily, finding comfort in the arms of her flesh and blood husband, buried her face in his shoulder.

"Hon, what's the matter? What do you want me to do?" They both sat down in the chairs in the room.

"This isn't right. We shouldn't defile my daughter's memory like this. We should stop."

"Are you sure, Em? I'll support you with anything you decide, but don't do this because you think that God is mad at you or anything."

"God? How can you talk about that now? This isn't about God. This is about losing my daughter! I want her to be a flesh and blood human. I want to have her memories of her untarnished by her being turned into a computer. Whatever comes out of there will never be like my memories of her. I'll always be comparing a machine to the memories of my little girl. Who am I doing this for? It's like when Buttons died. He was so old that he didn't want to go on. We were just keeping him on because of our selfish desires. Is this the same thing? Do I just want to hold on to her no matter what? Even though she'll never be the same?"

"Emily, please, think this through. Of course if you say so, I'll be behind you. I'll be with you. But this is something you can't ever take back. Once you stop the procedure it's all over, and Christine will be gone. Will you still feel this way a day, a week, or a year from now?"

Ralph was too terrified to say anything. He felt he should leave, but he couldn't take not knowing. He just stood there motionless.

"I'll never see her grow up and go to school. She'll never be a mother, she'll never have children."

"No, but she'll still be in your life. If you stop now, there is no going back."

"I don't know what to do. I just don't know."

"Em, really, honestly, I think you should go on. Let them finish."

"Really, Dave?"

"Yes. I don't know anything about being transcribed, but I know you. I love you and I love Christine. I think that you would someday regret stopping. I don't want to see that for you. I think that would hurt you more than having her transcribed."

"Dave, do you really mean that?"

"Yes, I do. I think it would tear you up inside. I think you would hate yourself not doing everything you could to save Christine."

"But is that really Christine in there? Will that still be her?" She looked at Ralph. "Are you still Ralph?"

"I feel like I am, Emily. I have all his memories and feelings. I still love Christine more than I can say. I would feel terrible to lose her now."

Emily shook her head, sighed and said, "All right, we'll go on. I can't know how she'll be. But I'll never know by stopping."

Ralph whispered, "Thank you, Em."

Turning to the door, Ralph said, "I'll leave you two alone. I'll be in the waiting room."

Ralph closed the door behind him as he headed down the hall, shaken to his core.

CHAPTER 6

Once the transcription has taken place, the Transcribed goes into what is called VR rehab. While it is not an actual place, it is a virtual reality where the Transcribed learn about their new life, their new brain, and how to use their new features and facilities. Also, they learn how seriously their life has changed and will never be the same.

Transcriptions have two broad categories, one where the patient is conscious throughout the process, and the other where it is done while the patient is unconscious.

There are advantages and disadvantages to both methods. In the first method, the conscious transcription, the patient is tested throughout the process to ensure that the Transcribed brain, as much as possible, is actually a true representation of the original brain. This reduces much of the post-transcription review that is performed before a permanent transcription license is issued. On the minus side, however, since the patient is conscious during the process, they can see and feel their body slowly being consumed as the nano-processors examine and extract their neurons from their body.

The process of transcription not only reduces their original brain to pulp, it also travels down the spine and extremities to extract major nerve bundles and create equivalent maps within the Transcribed support substrate. Without this part of the process, the Transcribed would be paralyzed. While quite painless, this can be quite traumatizing to watch.

The unconscious transcription proceeds much the same way in the mechanical process of examination, replacement, and discarding of each neuron. The patient, during *the process, for whatever reason, is unconscious. They are spared the endless testing that is performed. Also, after the initial trauma of the process has begun, the whole operation can take from six to twelve hours and can become quite tedious and boring. The unconscious patient is spared that tedium. However, the surgeon cannot have absolute assurance the nano-machines that have performed the bulk of the process have absolutely created an exact duplicate of the original neuron.*

As a result, the unconscious Transcribed is under a heightened level of scrutiny prior to being issued a permanent license. While both transcription methods use various types of checksums to ensure that the memories and functions of the original brain are correctly transcribed, there can be no positive assurance. So, the Transcribed is queried about their memories, life, and opinions post-operatively.

Now it would seem that the best way to be transcribed, despite the terror and tedium, would be the conscious method. While this is the preferred method, it is not always possible.

The VR environment that is created for the Transcribed post-operatively is a soothing, calm environment, devoid of any feelings that could excite the newly Transcribed.

The physical result of the process is a translucent cube, approximately thirty centimeters on a side, which represents the supporting computer substrate. And within the cube is a sphere that is the actual Transcribed brain, interfaced on a dendrite level with the substrate.

Attached to the cube, is a smaller fifteen-centimeter cube, which is the smart-plug that interfaces with the physical world. It represents the spinal cord and major neurons extracted from the patient and mapped into the Transcribed brain. It has its own computing substrate that facilitates the connection. The processing that is performed to convert the electrical signals to and from the Transcribed's brain to the mapped spine is considered a new and completely artificial brain cortex, called the "spinal cortex".

There are additional channels within the substrate and the physically Transcribed brain that allow the substrate to communicate with the brain, allow for heat extraction, and to allow for passage of replacement neurons as the original neurons wear out.

Once the operation is performed, the created brain is extracted from the surgical suite and enclosed in its armored casing. This provides physical support of the rather fragile computer that has been created. It also provides electrical and cooling connections to the support frame. The spinal cortex however is left exposed and is the actual smart plug component that attaches to the support frame providing connection to the outside world.

During this post-operative process, the Transcribed is rendered unconscious if they were awake. The computing substrate, which was given power and cooling by the surgical suite, is transferred to the support frame. Part of the process is to build a floor for the substrate to sit on. The bottom of this floor contains the connection to a low voltage maintenance power cell that is used to protect the substrate and the brain while it is detached from the mobile support frame. At no time during this process can the substrate be without power. If it does, the Transcribed essence is lost and the patient is dead. This is one of the most delicate parts of the operation.

Once the brain has been mounted on the mobile support frame it can be transferred to the rehab center. The rehab center is a computer room-like area where the newly Transcribed can be properly awakened into their new life. Their smart-plug spinal cortexes are mated to the computer room's internal network through smart-plug connectors.

The network provides a VR area where the Transcribed awakens in a calm atmosphere and begins the process of learning how their new brain works and prepares for re-integration into society.

Here is where loved ones can meet if desired. For many, this is a very traumatic time. If they were transcribed as a result of an accident, they may be completely unprepared for a life inside a box. Many of those initially feel that they have died and they are just shadows or ghosts of their previous selves. There are some few who regret their decision altogether and opt for termination. While their VR personas cannot physically die, of course, their underlying substrate can be powered off. This is the ultimate form of suicide. It is quick, painless, and irrevocable.

Of course, this option is not taken lightly and they receive extensive counseling before being given permission. But in the end it is their right to die.

The VR rehab environment is considered life with training wheels. Here the Transcribed wake to a place that is soothing and calm, where they cannot hurt themselves or others. Here they learn that they not only have extended their life expectancy, but they can experience life at a varying timescale so they could slow their minds down to watch a flower bloom or speed it up to view hummingbird wings in flight. Also, they can have, not just information, but knowledge, through the merest effort of thought. Without the need of the corrosive element called oxygen, their hardware can be mated to spaceships or submarines.

Since sleep is no longer a physical need, they can work tirelessly as long as their power cells hold out. While they *do need a period of time to rest to allow their brains to integrate their experiences into memories as their flesh and blood brains did, it only requires a few minutes of what would be called reflection or meditation to achieve the same level of mental acuity that their flesh bodies once needed hours for.*

-Life Without A Brain, The History of Transcription - 2177

Christine was taken, both physically and virtually to begin her new life as Transcribed.

Ralph had requested to be there when Christine was awakened to help ease her realization of what happened to her.

Ralph entered the VR rehab virtual area, which presented itself as a clinic. People both in street clothes and clinical outfits were walking around. After inquiring at an information kiosk he made his way to the ward where the newly Transcribed are initially awakened. Outside the ward, the doors were marked with warnings indicating that the ward was running over clocked and that time would pass slower for those outside. The recovery area was run in over clock so that the newly transcribed could speed their recovery. Often times, many days of counseling are required for the Transcribed to go through the five stages of grief to accept their new life.

Counselors, too, could spend more time with each patient and give them more fulfilling counseling while over clocked.

Ralph entered the ward and only saw one bed with Christine in it. That is the way the ward is presented. While there may be more than one patient in VR rehab, they are presented as a single patient initially so they may have privacy in their awakening. Eventually, they will enter group therapy and talk about their experiences with others in the same process as themselves.

Ralph walked over and stood next to Christine's bed. Christine appeared to be sleeping peacefully. The doctor that performed the transcription came up to Ralph. Since they are all in VR, they all appear in their pre-deceased body images.

"She has been successfully instantiated, Mr. Chalmers. She can be awakened whenever you like."

"Thank you, doctor. Were there any complications?"

"No, it went better than we were expecting. There was no cranial damage to speak of; her brain was completely intact. She should make a complete recovery. Have you given any thought to what body style she should have?"

"Frankly, no. This has been so sudden. We'll discuss it with her when the time comes."

"Very good. I'll leave you two alone. Her simulation is bound to the bed. Sometimes when a newly Transcribed wakes up, they start thrashing around from the shock. Of course she can't hurt herself."

"Thank you, doctor."

The doctor left the room.

Ralph leaned over his daughter and ran his hand over her head. He is pleasantly surprised to feel the individual hairs on her head and the warmth of her skin. Her image was constructed from pictures and videos of her, as well as what was reconstructed from her physical body form.

"Christine. Christine, can you hear me?" As if waking from a deep sleep, she seems to struggle to wake up.

"Chris, hon, wake up, it's me, Daddy."

With a groan, Christine twists on the bed and yawns, and then opens her eyes.

She looks at her father and sees him in his pre-deceased form and her eyes grow wide.

"Daddy?! Is that you? Oh, Daddy! Are you back?" She reached up and hugged her father. Ralph can feel her arms around his neck. He can feel her breath on his ear.

She let go of his neck and sits up in the bed. "Daddy! It was terrible! Dale reached for the package and it exploded and there was heat and then I... I... woke up here. Daddy, what happened?"

"Darling, it was terrible. More terrible than you can know. I am so sorry."

"Sorry for what, Daddy, what happened? Did something happen to Dale?"

"Yes, darling, Dale died in the explosion. They couldn't repair him."

"Oh no! He was so nice to me. Why would someone do that?"

"I'm afraid there are some very bad people in the world and they don't like people like us."

"Are you all right? Did you get hurt?"

"I'm fine, Honey. I had some damage to my chassis, but I'll get a new one."

"That's good. Why am I in the hospital, I didn't get hurt, did I? How long was I asleep?"

Ralph closed his eyes for a moment trying to gather the inner strength to speak the next words to his daughter.

"Honey, please understand. If there were anything else we could have done we would have done it. We had no choice. What we did, what your mother and I decided was for you, was to save your life."

"What? What did you do?"

"Darling, please. You were badly hurt in the explosion. You were badly burned. And pieces of the bomb blew through your body. The medics did all they could for you."

"Daddy, I don't understand. What happened?"

"Darling, we… we had them transcribe you. Your body was killed in the explosion there wasn't anything else we could do."

"What?" Christine looks around and suddenly the realization dawned on her. VR rehab starts as a hospital room on a sunny day with a mild breeze. The hospital room is neutrally appointed with no obvious technology. No beeping boxes or displays with wriggling lines. Preferably, the Transcribed wakes to a family member with them. If no one is available, then the doctor that did the transcription will wake the patient.

"No!!" she screams. "No! No! No! I don't want to be a robot! Everyone will make fun of me! They'll hate me! How can I ever go back to school? No one will recognize me!" Christine starts sobbing and starts thrashing on the bed, making fists with her hands and hitting the bed and rocking back and forth. She tries to sit up but is bound to the bed and cannot raise herself. Ralph leans over and holds his child.

She hugs her father and sobs into his shoulder. Telling her it will be all right, he soothes her. After a time her sobbing stops. She turns her head and sobs into the pillow.

Ralph sits down next to her.

"Why can't I move? I want to get out of here! I want to run away! I don't want to be like this!"

"Hon, you're bound to the bed, you can't get up yet. It's for your own good."

"I want to get up!"

"Christine, please settle down. If you calm yourself, I'll have you unbound and we can talk."

After a moment of seething, she settles down.

"Ok, I'm going to release you. You have to remain quiet."

Ralph calls up a control panel on his visual field and releases Christine.

"Ok, you can sit up now."

She sits up in the bed and looks at her hands and arms. She runs her hands over her arms and shoulders and feels her face. She looks down at her body covered by sheets and feels her torso and hips.

"Everything feels normal, like I was before. And Daddy! Your body! It's like your real body. The one you had before you had your accident."

"Yes, Hon. That is the way I think of myself. I don't think I'm a robot. I think of myself as you see me; a regular human with a human body. It makes things easier, really."

"So what about me, do I look human? Do I look like myself?"

"Certainly you do. Look!" Ralph produces a mirror from the table and shows it to Christine. She looks at herself in the mirror and touches her face.

"It's so strange. I don't feel any different."

"How did you expect to feel? Really that is the whole point of being Transcribed. You have a new brain, but you didn't change. And now you'll be able to do things you couldn't before. You'll never forget anything, unless you want to. Like the memories of the explosion. If you want, you can remove them or mute them or put them in a place where they can't hurt you. Also, you can learn just about anything just by thinking about it. You can download information from the net and have it integrated into your knowledge instantly. You can also think faster now. There are other things, but you'll learn them in time."

"What about Mom? Can I see her?"

"Soon darling, soon."

"Did she agree with you? She hated the church you started. David thinks you aren't human, that you died in the car accident."

"She didn't want you to die, Hon. We talked about it and we had very little time to make a decision. Your body was all but dead from the explosion. If we hadn't acted as fast as we did, you would have died. In the end, she agreed."

"But that would have been all right too, wouldn't it? I mean, I still would have gone to heaven, right? That's what you saw in your accident, wasn't it? You saw God."

"Yes darling, of course, but we still would have missed you terribly."

"When can I see her?"

"Well to you, it will be about a week, but to her it will be just a couple of hours."

"Why is that? I don't understand."

"It's called over clocking. Right now our brains are thinking faster than your mom's brain, so she can't come here just yet. We're doing this so you can get acquainted with your new brain. Then we'll meet in FIVR and we can have a picnic."

"You can eat here, too?"

"Sure, you can do anything you want."

"I never saw you eat when we were together. You always cooked for me but you never ate."

"Well my chassis is a mechanical thing that runs on electricity, it doesn't eat. But that doesn't mean I don't like food. I just do it in VR."

"There sure is a lot to learn."

"Yeah there is. But it will go quickly. You'll also have to practice using your new body. We'll start in simulation and after a while we'll go pick one out for you and you can practice using it."

"I'll have a chassis too, just like you."

"Yes, but you can pick your own options, within reason. A chassis is very expensive and will take a long time to pay for, but you can have some say in the matter. Your mother and I will have to discuss what options we have and then we can talk to you about it. You'll have some say in it, but you have to be reasonable."

"Can I get one with legs?"

"Darling, we'll talk about it later, but a fully humanoid chassis is really very, very expensive and not all that much better than something like what I have. You don't remember seeing that many of them at the church do you?"

"No, there were only a couple as I remember."

"There's a reason for that."

"Hey, does that mean I can go to communion now?"

"Yes, of course. Now you'll be able to see what all the others are seeing when they join me in the high bandwidth link."

"Can we commune now? Here?"

"I would rather you wait until we get back to the church. I want to have a memorial service for Dale. Also, we can't really do it here. Even though we're together in this room, our computing substrates are in different locations. The high bandwidth link only works when we're in a local network."

"You really saw God?"

"Yes, honey, I did. By the way, do you remember anything after the explosion and before you woke up just now?"

"No, not really, I felt like I was asleep until you woke me up. Why?"

"Just checking. I thought on the off chance you might have seen God, too. So far I'm the only one who is Transcribed to have had this type of experience."

"I wonder why that is, Daddy? Why hasn't anyone else seen God like you have?"

"No other Transcribed have, that's true. But others have had spiritual experiences, but they've always been flesh and blood people. Usually as the result of some sort of trauma like a heart attack or car accident."

"What happened to them?"

"Most of them describe being wrapped in a deep all powerful love. Some say they saw a bright light. But all of them feel they touched something deep and infinite, and all knowing."

"I didn't feel anything. What was it like for you?"

"Hon, it's awfully hard to describe. But it was glorious! When the accident happened, I felt myself being crushed by the car as it rolled over and over. Then when it stopped it was like I was floating above the car. I didn't feel any pain and all I could do was watch. The emergency team hadn't arrived by that point and all I could see was the car. I saw my body just sitting there, trapped in the car. I was thinking about us, how I would never see you again. I knew I was dead and I was just waiting for the end.

Then everything faded out and I was just in darkness. Then there was light. It just came over me in a rush. I felt comforting warmth. And love. I felt I was loved. But it was love that I cannot describe. It was like it penetrated every part of my being. Then God spoke."

"You've told me and spoke at church about what you and God said, but did you really speak to him?"

"Really, Hon, most of it I don't remember. We spoke about everything. We spoke about my whole life. About your mother and I, and you. We spoke about the things I've done. And the things I should have done."

"So God called you a sinner?"

"No, it wasn't that. Sin really isn't a concept that God uses. It's more a judgment I have against myself. I have sinned, not because God says what I did or didn't do was wrong, but *I* thought it was wrong. I stood in judgment of myself. I looked at all the things I had done and I knew they were sins. I was sinning at the time and I knew it and I did it anyway."

"So we make our own sin?"

"Something like that. But it is more. It's more that the sin is that I didn't have love in my heart and that was the sin."

"So did God say he was going to send you to Hell?""

"No, hon, I don't think there is a Hell. Just judgment. Because when I was finished confessing, we talked about the good things

I had done. All the times I have had love in my heart and used that love in my life."

"Then I felt the darkness in me disappear, like smoke in a storm. God had not only forgiven me, he had removed the darkness I carried."

"Daddy, I've known you all my life, I've never seen you do anything bad. You're not a bad man."

"No, I don't think so either. I never did anything evil, but everyone at some time in their lives is faced with decisions that they always regret. They take a path that they knew was wrong. Whether it was marrying the wrong person, or doing business that was against their better judgment. This is sin; this is the thing that is wrong. We are intelligent creatures; we have the ability to know right from wrong. We can investigate, we can search. We can decide, and we have to take responsibility for what we decide and do. But many times we don't."

"So all of that happened in a flash?"

"I don't know how long it lasted. All I have left are feelings and images."

"Then you woke up in here?"

"Well, not quite like you did. Before I woke up, God told me what He wanted me to do."

"That's when He told you to build the church?"

"No, He never said anything about a church and He never said anything about worship."

"Then why did you do it? Why did you start the church?"

"I didn't think I had any other way of Him telling me what He wanted. He said that the Transcribed were cut off from His love that is all. That I should tell them that He is there to love them. That is all."

"How are they supposed to do that? If they're the same as they were before, can't they just go back to their own church or something?"

"I don't know. All I know is what He said, and the gift. He left me a gift. A gift to share with all who want to receive it."

"That is what you felt when you woke up?"

"Yes, that's it. That brief second before I was instantiated in VR, I felt His glorious love. I felt the warmth. I was allowed to keep that memory, exactly as I felt it. I can relive those memories now that I am Transcribed. That is what I share in communion."

"So the other people in the church can relive them as well?"

"Yes, but you have to be Transcribed to get it. Through the high bandwidth link, we share the memories of that brief second of infinite love. Our sensoriums merge and we truly become one and that memory is gifted to those who commune."

"Now I can feel that when I go to church?"

"Yes, darling, giving you that gift would be the most precious thing I could ever give you."

"I would really like to do that, Daddy."

"You will, Honey, you will."

"So how soon can I go?"

"Well first, you have to finish rehab. After that the doctor has to check you out and get you a transcription license. Then we can get a chassis for you. Then you can come to the church and we'll have a celebration for you."

"What about the doctor? I have to get a license? Like a driver's license or something?"

"It's a little more complicated than that, Hon. But,no, you don't have to study for it. The doctor is just going to ask you some questions, that's all."

"What if I fail the test, do I have to take it again? What could go wrong?"

"Nothing is going to go wrong, really. It's just a formality we all have to go through."

"I don't understand. If it's a formality, why do we have to go through it?"

Ralph looks away and decides to be truthful to her daughter.

"Darling, sometimes, only in very bad cases of transcriptions, the doctor can't save the person. They examine them and they say that it didn't go right. And if they can't fix them, they don't want them to suffer. So they… they turn them off."

"Turn them off? What does that mean. That they die?"

"Yes, Hon, they die."

"They can do that? Why? Why would they kill someone?"

"Darling, transcription is a very complex thing and even though there are very few problems, sometimes, something goes wrong. Or the person is hurt too much and their body can't be recovered. And they try the transcription, but it doesn't work. It doesn't instantiate, then they have no choice."

"So is that what they're going to do with me? They're going to see if they have to turn me off? They're going to kill me?"

"Darling, really, it's nothing like that. In your case, everything went fine, there were no problems. I talked with the doctor and he was quite pleased with the way it went. He's just going to ask you some questions, that's all. Really."

"Oh, Daddy, I'm scared!"

"It's all right, Honey. It'll be all right." He hugs his daughter trying to soothe her fears.

"But the thing of it is, that once you get done. You're given a license and they can never question you again. You're legally considered as human as you ever were and no one can ever take that away from you."

"Never?"

"Not ever."

What Ralph didn't tell her is that his transcription was almost terminated. He was one of those whose transcriptions should never have even been attempted. He was dead when they tried to transcribe him. The doctors all recommended against even trying. But Emily was adamant. By all medical judgments, Ralph's transcription qualified as a miracle.

But too, he had to go through a much more rigorous review. He very nearly did not qualify for a license. He was very nearly terminated.

Emily, Christine and Ralph in VR (not FIVR), arrive at the doctor's office in the hall. They see the doctor's office door with his name emblazoned on it.

Christine turned to Ralph. "Dad, I'm scared."

"It's going to be all right, Hon, the doctor just wants to ask you a few questions. He has to make sure the operation went correctly, that's all." Emily flashes a look of worry, too, but said nothing.

"But if he says that it didn't go well, they'll turn me off! You have to tell him, Dad, I'm not a bad girl, I didn't do anything wrong! It's not my fault!"

Ralph put his arms around his daughter. "Christine, really, it's going to be all right. This is just a formality; the doctor was very pleased with the way everything went. They've never had a problem here. The doctor is one of the best at this."

They entered and saw the doctor sitting behind his desk.

"Good afternoon! Christine, it's wonderful to see you again! How are you feeling?"

"Fine, Doctor."

"Nervous?"

"Yes, a little," she answers hesitantly.

"My dear, really, this is just a formality. I'm afraid I must go through this because of the law. But I am quite sure everything will work out just fine."

"Did you have to go through this?"

"Not quite like this, no. My transcription was done while I was conscious and so the checking was done while I was awake.

But my transcription had to be validated as well. I know how nervous you are."

"Will it hurt?"

"Hurt? No, my dear, all I'm going to do is ask some questions. You'll give me the answers as best as you can. That's really all. I'm going to ask your parents some questions also to see how their memories compare with yours. But not about the same things. The process is called check summing. It comes from the old days of computers when they would send data from machine to machine and they wanted to make sure that the data wasn't corrupted in the transmission. During those days it was a simple mathematical algorithm, but for transcriptions, it a bit more involved, but basically the same."

"How can you check my memories?"

"Well, we don't really check them as much as we know the data that was gathered during the operation. We can check much of that data in your computer and compare them to make sure that they match within certain bounds."

Emily says, "Doctor, can we get on with this, please? We've all been through so much trauma these last few days that we don't need any more of it!"

"Of course, I'm sorry. Let's begin. Ok, Christine, do you recall your fifth birthday?"

"Let me think. Oh yes, I do. Daddy and Mom had a cake with my name on it and there was a candle in the middle of the cake in the shape of the number five."

"Good, do remember what color the cake was or what flavor?"

"I think it was white with green and blue trimmings. It was chocolate."

"Good. Did you get any presents for your birthday?"

"Yes, I got presents from Mom and Dad, and my aunt sent a card with a gift card in it, and my grandma came by later and brought me a toy robot poodle that would follow me around and play fetch with me."

"Good, very good. Now was there something special that you remember about that day?"

Christine immediately says "Oh, yes! In the middle of the party, the doorbell rang and I went to answer the door. Outside there were five carolers singing Christmas songs. I thought it was rather strange because my birthday is in May. Then when they got done singing, they gave me a present. It was a very tall box wrapped in paper with Easter bunnies on it. And when I opened the present there was a doll that was just as tall as I was! And when I opened the box she sat up and opened her eyes and said 'Happy Birthday, Christine!' and we played together for the rest of the day!"

Ralph and Emily look at each other horrified.

Good!" said the doctor. "Now Christine, I want you to think very hard and try to remember exactly what happened that day."

Christine gets a look of concentration on her face. "Doctor, I don't know why I said that, I don't remember that at all. That never happened!"

"No, it didn't Christine. We did that during the operation."

Emily and Ralph look surprised. "What? I don't understand," said Emily.

"It's called an implanted memory. It's part of the checksum process. We implanted this nonsensical memory in Christine's mind during the procedure for just this purpose. It is one of the ways that we can be sure that the memories were transferred correctly. It's what's called a "one-use memory". Now that Christine thinks of it, the memory disappears and all that is left is her memory just now about saying it."

Ralph said, "I don't recall anything like that during my review."

"Your case was highly unusual. We were so concerned with getting the data out that we didn't want to implant any false memories. Your process was much more fragile and delicate. But you did go through a much higher level of scrutiny."

"Yes, that I do remember!"

"Ok, let's go on. Christine what do you want to do when you grow up?"

"Well, I thought about it and I've always liked working with animals, and I was hoping to become a vet or a vet's assistant."

"I'm sure that you'll do very well at it if you try," said the doctor.

The questions went on like this for about fifteen minutes between Christine and the doctor. He asked some questions to which Christine can't answer, and once Ralph tries to help by prompting Christine and the doctor cuts him off.

"Please, Mr. Chalmers, don't prompt her. It's not so much that she remembers details or facts; it's the way she remembers or doesn't remember things. The brain is a very complex system and is constantly reorganizing memories. As she answers the questions, I'm watching her brain analyze and operate on a display in my visual field. Some memories are forgotten while others are remembered. That is completely normal so that Christine's responses have to be honest and not forced."

After a few more questions, the doctor turned to Emily and Ralph, "Now I'm going to ask you some questions about what you remember about Christine. Ralph, do you remember what Christine said to you when you first came home after your transcription?"

"Yes, she asked if I was in Tokyo," he said, smiling at the memory. Since he has been Transcribed, his memory is much sharper now and he can recall those moments quite vividly.

"Emily, do you recall what happened when you had to put down your cat?"

"Yes, Christine cried for days. Buttons was very old, almost twenty-five, but he could no longer endure any more age extension treatments and it was best to let him pass. I was heartbroken, too. I'd had him since I was a teenager."

"Did she say anything in particular that you recall?"

"Yes, as we were going to take him to the vet's for the last time, she held him tightly and said, 'You rest now, Buttons, I'll see you when I get to heaven,' Emily said and she turned her head to hide the tears.

The doctor asked questions back and forth for another half an hour, sometimes asking Christine, sometimes asking her parents. As they answered the questions, they could see the doctor's eye tracking data on his visual field. Since it was only for the doctor, it was invisible to the three of them. Because of that, he gives the appearance of being distracted while they are answering the questions put to them.

Finally the doctor said, "Ok, I think we have enough. I've been scoring the results as we went through the questions, and let me assure you that Christine has passed completely. I will submit my findings and she will be issued her permanent transcription license."

Christine had a big smile on her face and Emily and Ralph let out a sigh of relief.

"Thank you, Doctor, thank you!" said Emily.

"Really, I didn't expect any problems, as far as these things go, it was routine. Its cause was horrific, of course, but the process was nothing out of the ordinary."

After some brief goodbyes, they left the doctor's office and stood back in the hallway.

"Well, I guess we can start looking at chassis for you, Chris," said Ralph.

"That sounds really nice, when can we go, Dad?"

"One step at a time. Your father and I still have some things to work out, but we'll come to that soon enough."

"Em, what do we need to talk about?"

"Well, first off, financing! How are we going to pay for it?"

"I've been working on that. I'm trying to work out a loan from the church. It will be fine."

"And what about visitation? She still lives with me, you know, and is only supposed to visit with you. Even though we've had a falling out with the church, I don't want you to think that she's going to be living with you from now on!"

"Emily, please! Nothing has changed. I'm not going to take Christine away from you. Yes, right now she and I will be spending quite a lot of time together to get her used to her new life, but you're still her mother, I would never try to take that away from you."

"When can she come back to our house? How soon can you get her a chassis?"

"Assuming I can get the loan, and we can find a chassis that she likes and we can afford, maybe about another week to ten days. But then there'll be a day or so to have her mated with the chassis and some real world training. Once we pick one out, she can start practicing with a sim."

"The house seems empty right now, I miss having my little girl around," she said, as she affectionately tousled Christine's hair. Emily thought to herself, *I'll never be able to do that anywhere but here from now on.*

"Give me a call tomorrow, Ralph, and we'll talk some more about it."

"Ok."

"What are you two going to do now?"

"We're going to have some ice cream to celebrate!" said Christine.

"That's right! You can do that in here. You're so lucky! You can eat as much as you want and never put on an ounce!" said Emily with a smile.

Suddenly Emily looked up at them. "Well, I have to go. I have an appointment with my doctor this afternoon; just the regular check up. I'll talk to you tomorrow!"

With that, Ralph and Christine see Emily reach up to her face with both hands, as she seems to grab an invisible helmet. As she lifts the helmet off, Emily disappeared.

Emily removed the helmet from her head and is back in her darkened bedroom, lying on the bed. She places the helmet on the bedside table and takes off the haptic gloves, which allowed her to feel what she touched in VR and set them next to the helmet. Then she turned on her side and sobbed quietly into her pillow.

CHAPTER 7

It has been said that the relationship a Transcribed person has with their chassis is similar to the relationship a cowboy has with their horse. A horse anticipates his rider's needs and only subtle hints are needed to understand what direction their rider wants to go.

So, too, is it with a chassis. More than simply a cart to move the Transcribed's brain-box around, it provides important support functions such as generating and storing electrical energy. It provides the necessary cooling that is generated by the operation of the computer substrate. It interprets the myriad signals that the brain generates for body movement. So, for example, the unconscious way that a person gestures with their arms as they speak is given lifelike actualization by the chassis. Also, a person has legs, but most chassis use treads or wheels. The chassis will interpret the act of walking, by the Transcribed, into movement. The chassis provides tactile feedback to the Transcribed from the sensation of touch. Though primarily located in the fingers and hands of the chassis, it can also sense when any part of the chassis has been touched. So, too, is the sensation of temperature as related back to the computer substrate. Also, there are cameras located in the upper portion of the chassis at face level that provides stereoscopic vision. But unlike simple digital video cameras, these image sensors provide data much like the human eye, in a way that is similar to the way that the retina sends data to the visual cortex.

There is a screen on top of the chassis that is used to provide a vision of the face of the Transcribed. This also is interpreted by the facial nerves that provide expression through the facial muscles. However, if a Transcribed wishes to have anonymity, the screen can display simple "screen savers" or play videos.

Stereo microphones provide hearing. But, here again, these are not simple microphones, but sophisticated audio processors that interpret the sound in a way that is similar to that of human hearing and that data is presented to the computer substrate's audio cortex.

All of this is accomplished by a very sophisticated AI that coordinates the actions of the disparate parts of the chassis, monitors the status of the parts and the computer substrate, and provides this information to the Transcribed as either visual information that is superimposed over their visual field, or as subtle body sensations such as feeling the texture of the floor the treads are resting on, or as a feeling of hunger when the power starts to dip. A feeling of exhaustion will be felt if the chassis or motors start to overheat.

The chassis has storage cells for power that can be charged either from standard electrical mains or from solar cells that are integrated in the chassis.

The body itself is coated with an active nano-coating that can be used to change the apparent color of the chassis, body, and head. Additionally, patterns can be displayed so fashion can be exhibited, allowing Transcribed people to differentiate themselves if they wish.

The chassis also provides access to the radio spectrum for wireless communication for the Transcribed. It can also signal for help if there is a problem. An autonomous mode is usually used during maintenance when the Transcribed may be disconnected from their chassis. This allows the maintenance technicians to work on the chassis and direct its operation remotely. This is a physical switch within the chassis body and *can't be enabled without the permission of the Transcribed. This prevents an unauthorized user from hijacking a chassis, causing it to go on a rampage.*

Enhanced vision or hearing isn't really possible for the Transcribed any more than it is for a flesh and blood human. The reason isn't technological as it is physical. The human brain, whether silicon or flesh, has a visual cortex that has been evolved over millions of years to interpret visual signals from a narrow band of photons. Extending that range into the infrared or ultraviolet just can't be interpreted by the brain. However, the band of visual data can be offset in one direction or another, so they can see into those spectrums, but they lose the ability to see what is in the area that was offset from.

Same with hearing, you can offset the range of audio information, but you lose the ability to sense data from the lower range.

There are certain enhancements that are possible such as magnification of vision or sounds. But they are not superman with x-ray vision and preternatural hearing ability.

The strength of the chassis is limited to the efficiency of the motors used to enable movement. They can move a fairly high pace for a short distance before the motors start to overheat. They can also grip somewhat harder than a human, but they cannot bend steel.

The chassis body itself is hardened and the container within the chassis that houses the computer of the Transcribed is enshrouded in armor as well, much like the cranium completely houses the brain to protect it. This provides protection from most types of accidents. That is why the chassis and the computer both maintain primary and secondary power support. The chassis power storage is much higher. The computer substrate maintains a low voltage maintenance power cell that can provide anywhere from one to four hours of backup, but in this state, the computer is non functional and the personality within is unconscious. It can provide support until emergency services can attach a backup diagnostic plug, which supplies power and communication to the computer.

Part of the integration into society was the implementation of emergency engineering support in major population centers that had a number of Transcribed. Much like emergency medical personnel, they are trained on the basic design and support of the Transcribed and how best to provide help in the case of a problem.

In less developed areas where there are fewer Transcribed, this support is provided by cross-trained medical techs.

Much of the support usually just requires the quick diagnosis of the problem, attaching the diagnostic plug, and transporting to an engineering center for repair. Fortunately, in most cases, once power is resupplied to the computer, the individual is out of immediate danger and the technicians can take a more relaxed approach to assessing the issues.

The process of integrating a Transcribed person to a chassis is called "mating". The chassis AI has to learn all the subtle signals that the person uses to interact with the real world. So, too, the Transcribed person has to learn and understand the information that is presented to them from the chassis. It is quite a bit more than just hooking up the cables. This mating process pairs the Transcribed to their chassis. So one Transcribed person cannot use the chassis from another Transcribed person without going through the mating process.

This has lead to the development of both industrial and military products that are designed for being mated to the Transcribed. For example, a Transcribed enabled "mate-able" crane can be operated by a Transcribed person by visualizing the movement of their arm to move the crane, and closing or opening their hand as opening and closing the crane's claw.

The military also has Transcribed driven vehicles such as troop carriers and tanks. Being mated to a flying vehicle has not had as much success. Apparently, trying to integrate all of the controls into the Transcribed sensorium is more difficult than simply having a flesh and blood pilot, so other than experimental aircraft there are no Transcribed people flying solo.

The first trans-mated device after the chassis was the surgical equipment that is used to transcribe a brain. It consists of multiple end effectors that the surgeon can activate by going through the motions of putting an arm in a sleeve. It also allows the surgeon to better supervise the process of transcription, as information from the nano-robots that perform the actual interpretation of the neuron they convert, is sent to the surgeon for review.

All this sophistication and support comes at a high price. That is the reason for the incredible cost of transcription; easily costing as much as a house. Financing a chassis became an important part of the financial industry as a result. Mortgages for chassis easily extend decades, and these costs are accepted by Transcribed as their lifespan has been indefinitely extended. So a few decades of cost is easily borne. There are costs associated with maintenance and support that are on top of mortgage fees, just like heating and electricity are additional costs to owning a house.

While defaulting on a mortgage is possible, of course, foreclosure really isn't possible. If a Transcribed defaults, they can be extracted from their chassis and have it repossessed. The Transcribed is housed (stored) in a maintenance facility much like a computer room where their substrates are stored in racks. They are provided with network access and *can use a remote to go out in the world, but don't have the range of movement or the wealth of sensation that is provided by a chassis. This allows them interaction with society while they get their finances in order and when they become solvent again, their maintenance costs while housed are added to their mortgage costs.*

As with houses, cars, and just about any other man made item, there are markets for both new and pre-owned chassis. Though the costs are still high, a previously used, reconditioned re-mateable chassis can defer costs. The used market isn't quite as brisk as it is for other items, because once a person acquires a chassis they tend to keep it for quite a long time. However, there are those who upgrade to the newest and best chassis, just to be on the leading edge.

-Life Without A Brain, The History of Transcription - 2177

So it was when Ralph took Christine to look for a chassis. Available options are usually limited to increased range from better energy storage to faster, more lightweight motors for better speed. There are some whose range of vision and hearing can be offset to very high or low ranges, but unless one expects to use those options, they are rarely bought.

There are chassis that have wheels and there are chassis that are humanoid. This last is top of the line material. Costing at the very top of the range, they can have lifelike skin that is warm to the touch and full sensation all over the body. The face can be modeled on the Transcribed's original face or anyone else or have a neutral visage. The skin tone can be adjusted to any that is desired and the gender can also be adjusted. However, these chassis have very little room for the Transcribed's computer and all the support equipment, so while lifelike, buying one is considered vain.

Ralph and Christine went to the virtual showroom for chassis. They met with the salesman and learned about Christine's need for a chassis. Ralph was also in need of a new chassis as well as his previous chassis was destroyed in the explosion. And while there was some salvage value, there wouldn't be much discount in the destroyed machine.

Ralph's new chassis would be provided by the insurance his mortgage offered and give him a replacement that was substantially the same as the one he had. Since he had previously owned a chassis there was no need to do a test drive of go through the requisite training.

For Christine, however, this was all new and she stared at each of the available models.

"I don't know what to look for, or what I want."

"Well, Hon, it is more practicality than flash. Think about the difference between wheels and treads, for example. Treads have a better time on different types of pavement, but wheels can go faster."

"I still want to look like a girl!"

"Hon, that's not really possible unless you pick one of the humanoid models. In VR, of course, you can look like whatever you want. And even in a chassis, you'll still be my little girl."

"These all look like something out of a science fiction movie."

"We can't help that, this is what we are now. We can't really get a human body."

"Couldn't they clone one? They can clone everything else."

"Yes, you could clone an entire human. But our brains are much larger than flesh and blood brains. They would never fit inside the body, as there's no room for the support equipment and the organs."

"I'm going to look like a robot."

"Hon, we've been through this. Please, the sooner you get a chassis, the sooner you can go back to the real world. And too, you'll hardly feel the difference once you're mated. You'll feel yourself walking and talking just like you did before. It feels very natural."

The salesman said, "Yes, it's all very natural. We'll go through an adjustment process when you are mated so that you have every sensation you had before. You'll interact with the real world in almost the same way you did."

"Ok, let's get this over with. How do I get in this thing? I'm not even the same size. There's no hatch."

"The simulation will envelop you and you'll feel like you are mated. If you are ready, I'll connect you to the simulator. From there you can try the various models and options."

"Ok, I'm ready, I guess."

"Very good." The salesman moved his hands in mid air, obviously manipulating controls in his field of vision.

"You'll get an inquiry from me asking to be allowed to connect to your sensorium. Please accept it."

Christine looks to be reading something in mid air, then presses a button next to what she is reading.

"Very good, thank you. Now I'm going to put you in one of the treaded models with basic controls. You'll feel like you've moved back to the showroom floor and your point of view will change slightly."

"Ok," she said.

With that Christine vanishes from the chair. Ralph and the salesman walk into the showroom to find Christine superimposed on one of the chassis. "Hey, I jumped!"

"Yes, your sensorium is now in the chassis. We can see you as well."

"Wait, something is wrong, I can't move and when I move my arms, the chassis arms don't move."

"I haven't enabled the controls yet. I'll start with the arms and torso."

He manipulates one of his invisible controls. "Ok, try moving your right arm slowly up and down. The sim is in training mode and will attempt to interpret your signals."

Christine slowly lifts her arm and the chassis right arm rises as well.

"Ok, now lift your wrist and slowly move each of your fingers starting with the thumb." Christine does this and the chassis mimics her movements.

"Hey, that's pretty cool!"

"Ok, now move your right arm in a circle and at the same time wiggle your fingers. This is to make sure that the sim tracks simultaneous movement."

Christine does that and the chassis follows flawlessly.

"Now let's do the left arm. Lift just like we did before."

Christine and the salesman continue through the training process for her upper body and in just a few minutes the chassis torso is moving in concert with the natural movements of Christine.

"Now we'll get to walking. I'll enable the treads, but I want you to stand absolutely still. If you move your legs, you could inadvertently cause the chassis to jump. Naturally nothing bad will happen, but you could bounce off the walls."

"Ok," she said.

"All right, now I want you to balance on your left foot and bend and lift your right leg. The chassis shouldn't move, but it will learn your balancing and leg movements."

"Why do I have to worry about balance? I'll be riding in a chassis with treads. It's not like I'm going to fall over."

"No, but balance is an integral part of walking. So the chassis will be able to pick up how you want to move by interpreting the way you balance and lean."

"I didn't know that."

"Yeah, it's a thing. Now lift your left leg the same way."

Christine balances on her other foot and lifts her leg.

"Ok. Now take one step forward, starting on your right foot."

Christine does that and the chassis moves with her.

"Now take one step with your left foot." The chassis follows her again. "Good. We're just about done with this part. Now turn and walk toward me." As she walks, the chassis follows her, but in fits and starts.

"Hmm, I think we have a slight timing problem. Please stand still." The salesman manipulates other invisible controls. "Ok, now try walking in circles." Christine does that and the chassis keeps up with her easily.

"Very good now try walking around the showroom."

Christine starts walking around and the chassis keeps up with her. As she gets nearer to one of the other chassis, a loud gong is heard.

"You bumped into that chassis. Nothing was damaged, of course, since we're in VR, but in the real world you'll have to be aware of your surroundings. Your chassis will be bigger than your old body, so you have to be more careful."

"I don't want to roll over someone's toes either."

"No you don't. The chassis will give you a signal when you start getting close. It'll feel like a little tickle sensation on the side you're nearest to something."

"Yeah, I did feel that, I just didn't know what that meant."

"I didn't tell you because I didn't want to give you too much information too soon."

"I wanted to ask you. What happens if I do tip over? How can I get up?"

"The chassis has a very low center of gravity so tipping isn't too much of a worry, even when turning at high speed. However, it can happen, especially on inclines or rough terrain. Part of your training will include what to do if that happens."

"Well, what can I do?"

"There are a couple of options. You can enable semi-autonomous mode and the chassis will assist you to right yourself, usually by extending your arms and spinning your treads. Also, at the base of the chassis is a rod that extends to assist with getting back upright. Sometimes however, your chassis could be damaged when you are tipped. If that occurs, the chassis will call for assistance. In that case the best thing to do is to just wait until help arrives."

"Does that happen often?"

"Not really. Though some thugs think it's funny to try to push a chassis over. That's why tipping is considered a form of assault and they can be prosecuted for it."

"I've heard of that, I never really knew what it meant."

"Yes, unfortunately, society still has its share of dark characters."

Christine continued to walk around the showroom, now avoiding getting too close to things.

"Hey! This feels just like walking! There's nothing to it!"

"I told you, didn't I?" said her father.

"If you try different chassis, now that we have the basic training done, you won't have to go through that again. You'll just move and everything should work just as you are now."

"I want to try the humanoid!"

"Ok, but I will warn you that it's not like walking around in a flesh and blood body."

"Why not?"

"For one thing, your point of view changes quite a bit and balance depends on your vision as much as your sense of feeling from your cochlea. The first time you enter it, you'll be surprised and your body will over-react. You very well may fall."

"I still want to try it," said Christine petulantly.

"I tried it too, Christine. I think everyone does."

The humanoid, while built along human form, was, because of physical constraints, taller than a regular human. Standing well over two meters tall, it was an imposing site.

"Ok, I'm going to move you to the humanoid, but I'm going to keep everything locked until you get a feeling for your new size. Here in VR, your head will appear in place of the standard one, but you can have any configuration you want."

Suddenly, the humanoid's head disappears and Christine's head is in its place.

"Hey! Where are my arms? I can't see them!"

"Since the humanoids arms are so much longer than yours, you have to learn that your reach is much longer. Seeing your regular arms would confuse you. Ok, I'm going to unlock the torso and upper body. But the legs are still locked and it is in auto balance mode. Put your hands on your hips and bend at the waist."

Christine slowly moves her arms. Before she puts them on her hips, though, she holds her hands in front of her and turns them over, examining them.

"Pretty neat, huh? Ok, now put your hands on your hips and bend over."

She puts her hands on her hips and starts to bend forward. To compensate the humanoid pushes its backside to the rear.

"Now straighten up and lean to your left and right. Notice the humanoid automatically leans in the opposite direction."

Christine does so and then straightens up.

"Now what?"

"I'm going to release the auto legs, but leave auto balance engaged. I want you to take one small step forward. The humanoid will assist you in the move."

Christine tries to move, but starts to flail her arms. The humanoid takes a stumbling step forward.

"Different, wasn't it?"

"Yeah, it felt like I was going to fall."

"That's the thing about walking. It's a constant fall and compensating to catch yourself. Ok now I'm going to turn auto balance off. Just stand there for a second and try to keep your own balance."

When the salesman presses one of his controls, Christine rocks forward then adjusts herself and stands upright.

"Good, very good! A lot of people tumble over when I turn auto balance off. Ok, now try to take a small step forward."

Christine concentrates and balances her weight on her left foot and lifts her right foot slightly then leans forward bringing her right leg up. Then she straightens up and pulls her left leg forward.

"Not bad for the first time! Do you think you can take a few steps now?"

"Sure! Watch me!"

Christine takes a few hesitant steps forward, and then starts to take longer and longer strides walking around the showroom.

"You want to try running?"

"You bet!"

"Ok, hold on. Stand still for a moment."

Suddenly the showroom disappears and they appear on a running track.

"Ok, take it for a spin! Just be careful in the turns. You only have to lean slightly to turn as you are running."

Christine nods and starts running down the track. First at a trot then faster and faster as her longer legs eat up the distance. Soon she is running as fast as the humanoid is capable of. As she is rounding one of the turns, she over compensates and trips and falls and tumbles to the ground. Ralph and the salesman run up to her. She is sitting on the ground, her hair is somewhat disheveled, but she is uninjured.

"How did that feel?"

"Weird. I could feel myself falling and suddenly a lot of indicators appeared, and then everything started to move in slow motion. I tried to keep from falling, but I couldn't stop myself. I felt like I was moving in molasses."

"When a chassis starts to experience distress, such as falling or tipping, it will automatically overclock you and flash alerts. This gives you extra time to try to help yourself, but you have to take into account that your body still can only move at a certain speed, so it feels sluggish. If you choose to have a humanoid chassis, you'll receive extra training because of that."

"Seems odd to have to do that, considering we started with a humanoid form," said her father.

"Yeah, but it's the difference between having a real body and the mechanical equivalent where we get into trouble."

"Ok, one last thing. Try running again as fast as you can. But this time I'm going to add the actual energy drain coefficients that you would have if you had a real humanoid body. This track is 800 meters around. See how many times you can run around it."

"Ok," she said.

"All right, stand up and start running."

Christine stood, took a runner's stance and started running. She completed one full circuit, but soon after completing the circle she starts to slow down, and after completing about a quarter of the next cycle she stumbles to a halt and starts to walk back. By time she returns, she is panting.

"Why am I so tired? I can't catch my breath!"

"That is the feedback that the chassis gives you, to say that the energy from the power cells is draining quickly and the motors are overheating."

"That wasn't very far."

"No, it wasn't. That's because we can't put the same amperage cells in the humanoid form as we do with the treaded chassis. Also, the motors and actuators are smaller and don't have the same torque, so they overheat much faster. Let's return to the showroom, now, shall we?"

"Ok."

The track disappears and they return to the showroom. Christine is no longer in the humanoid body and is standing with Ralph and the salesman.

"That was fun, but I still don't know what I want."

"Christine, much of it has to do with what we can afford as much as what you want. I think we should go with a pretty much standard chassis without any options. As you go along if you want to upgrade or change when you can afford it, you'll be able to," said her father.

"I agree. When you are just starting out it makes sense to learn how you will deal with things in your new life. You'll have plenty of time to make changes later. You don't want to pay for something that you won't really use."

"*I* have to pay for it?" she said incredulously.

"Not at first, Hon. From the loan I'm getting from the church and the donations from the parishioners, much of the mortgage will be paid for up front. But there will be ongoing costs that you'll eventually have to pay. I'll pay for them now, but when you get older, you'll have to get a job and pay for them yourself."

"How long will I have to be paying?"

"I'd have to run the numbers, but anywhere from twenty-five to fifty years."

"That long?"

"Hon, realize the one thing about being Transcribed is that you can live for more than one hundred and fifty years easily; possibly longer, perhaps as long as you care to. You see, these chassis can be upgraded as they wear out, and also the computer that is your brain can be replaced. There actually may come a time when you may be able to transcribe yourself back to a flesh and blood brain so you can have a flesh and blood body. The technology is improving year after year, so having a mortgage that is *only* twenty to fifty years means very little."

"I really didn't think about that part of it."

"Yes, it's a big change."

"How about we put together a chassis for you that has just the standard options. Realize that standard options still have some enhancements you didn't have before."

"Like what?"

"Well you can see further into the infra red or ultra violet and your range of hearing can be augmented as well. Not a lot, but enough to allow you to see the heat generated by someone or hear what a dog hears."

"Ok, let's get this started. Christine, the salesman and I will work through the options and costs then we'll show you what we came up with. You'll be able to test drive it completely and if you like it, we'll get it sim'd up and you can start to go through complete user and mating training."

"What can I do in the meantime?"

"If you want, just go back to the house and I'll call you when we're done." Ralph was referring to their virtual home, which actually looked more like a mansion than a house. Virtual real estate cost nothing more than the electrons to create its qubits.

"Why don't you call your mother and have a visit?"

"Sure, I can tell her about driving a chassis."

"I'm sure she'd like that. Tell her I'll come and talk with her about what I've found and we can talk about it.

"Ok, I'll be at the house," and with that, Christine vanished.

Ralph turned back to the salesman. "While we're here we can talk about getting a replacement chassis for me, as well."

"I'm sure we'll be able to find something for you, too."

They continued talking about prices, options, and availability.

Ralph and the salesman came to an agreement for a chassis. It was a pre-owned, basic chassis with just slightly above average tread motors, full AI integration, vision and audio in the standard range, with no offset ability. The cost was exorbitant, but well within the range that Ralph could afford with the loan from the church.

The Church of the Transcribed immediately opened a trust fund for Christine upon hearing about the attack. Their outpouring of sympathy and support was overwhelming to Ralph. The congregation gave sufficiently to afford the down payment and mating costs for her. The goal was reached within hours of the attack.

Ralph was provided for also. When the congregation found out that Ralph's chassis had been destroyed, they contributed to his discretionary fund with the proviso that he spend the money on his repairs. The mortgage insurance that he carried would cover most of the replacement, but there were ancillary charges associated with the customization of the chassis that weren't covered.

Ralph had previously gone to the dealer that put together his first chassis and made arrangements for his replacement and mating.

Ralph returned to the VR mansion and found Christine talking to Emily.

"Daddy, you're back! What did you come up with?"

"Yes, Ralph, what did you find?" Emily's tone was somewhat cynical, giving Ralph the impression that Emily was somehow cut out of the selection process, even though she declined to participate.

"It's a pretty basic model, Hon, but it is quite capable and should be fine for you. Later, if you want, you can get upgrades, but for right now this will be what you need."

"Do you have any pictures, Dad?"

"More than that, I brought a brochure that talks about the specific one you're going to get. Here, take a look."

Ralph triggered a file he had that presented a three dimensional presentation in mid-air about the chassis that had full audio and experiential information.

The file is interactive and since Ralph put earnest money down, he also had a sim file for Christine, so she could practice driving the chassis.

"When you're ready, you can start practicing with the sim. It's already trained for you from the files that were generated at the showroom. Each practice session will be recorded and used to help mating with the real one."

"How do I run the sim?"

"I'll send you the file and when you trigger it, you'll enter a VR training area that'll have a track that will get more complex as you go through the training sessions. You should probably overclock through those so you can pick up your chassis sooner."

"How long will the training take?"

"The basic training, which will get you through most issues, will take about two hundred experiential hours. Meaning it'll be two hundred hours to you, but wall clock time would be shorter if you overclock."

"But I'll feel like it's two hundred hours no matter what. That seems like a lot of time."

"Yes, it is. Having a chassis is about as close as getting a new body as you can get. Remember what it was like when you were a child and were learning to walk."

"I don't remember those times that much. I just remember falling down the stairs a lot."

"Yes, you did, but you did learn. It's much like that."

"I'll be able to climb stairs?"

"Yes, stairs, ramps, just about anything that you can roll on, you should be fine. The treads use gecko technology to grab the surface that you're rolling on. About the only thing you can't do is climb a ladder."

"And go swimming," said Chris dejectedly.

"You'll sink like a stone if you go into water. But you can be immersed for up to the limit of your battery power with no real problem."

"What if I do fall in the water?"

"Just roll out. The AI will locate you in the body of water you're in and direct you to the best route to roll out."

"I'd have a problem in a swimming pool."

"Yes, no swimming pools for you. But if you do, just find a safe location to stay and have the AI call for help."

"I liked swimming."

"Well, just create a swimming pool here and do all the swimming you like."

"It's not like real life."

"You'll feel it is. The sim of the pool can be made to behave in a completely life-like way. Even giving you chills if you get too cold."

The service at the Church of the Transcribed is a different experience to the Transcribed who attend, as opposed to those non-Transcribed who visit. While the external images are the same, something else entirely happens during communion.

Communion, like in other practices of religion, is the culmination of the Mass. It is the spiritual meal that the communicants have been prepared for during the Mass.

Likewise, it is the same for the Transcribed. The convocation, the songs, the sermon, all have lead to this point. This is the point that one is put in touch, however infinitesimally, with the Divine, the Infinite.

The communicant, however, for the Transcribed opens his memories to his sensorium. He relives the initial seconds of his instantiation in VR. In others, the earliest memories that they have of their resurrection are like waking from a deep, dreamless, sleep. They have no memories of what occurred during their transcription. However, for Ralph, there is something more. Something divine. Not divinity itself, but the echo; like that of a tolling bell. But, all that touch the sensorium of Ralph Chalmers feel that same echo. All that touch that memory are changed. For, at last, faith and truth are united.

The link is then broken and the communion is over. The Mass ends and all the communicants go their separate ways.

There is a built in one-minute timer in the token ring switch to break the link in order to prevent any possible issues during communion. None have ever occurred, but when Ralph was working with the designers of the link, they knew they could not conceive of every possible problem that would occur, so they installed a fail-safe, just in case.

Regardless, the link only lasts a few seconds. The link fragments on its own. It is not because of any action on any-one's part. It just stops. No one really knows why. They would prefer to have that communion with God just a bit longer. They speculate that God does not want the communicants to become enraptured.

A week has gone by in real time. But for Christine, who has spent this time overclocked, it has been more like a month. Ralph has spent most of this time with Christine helping her to adapt to her new life and learn how to use her new chassis both in sim and in reality. Much like learning to drive a car, so too, does it take practice to learn how to wear a chassis.

Near the end of the week, Christine and Ralph return to Ralph's apartment at the church.

"On Sunday, I'll lead the mass for the first time since the explosion. I would like you to be my acolyte and to join us in communion."

"I always wanted to join in that, but I couldn't before. That's the one thing about being Transcribed that I envied."

"Thank you, Chris. That means an awful lot to me. For you to experience that with me is deeply touching. God is so close to us now."

They hug and while it is a little awkward, it is heartfelt.

The next morning they go down to open the church. This time however, they check the security cameras that have been installed since the bomb exploded. Also different this time is that Dale Evers isn't there to meet them when they open.

As there is no physical space to prepare for church, there really isn't much to do other than wait for the congregants to arrive.

While they wait, Ralph and Chris go over the mass in VR. Ralph reviews the songs that will be sung and asks Chris to change the stain glass windows to something more appropriate for the season.

She goes up to the nearest window and reviews the available options. She chooses the rosette at the front of the church from the Church of the Basilica in Rome. The others are more contemporary, and for a change she picks the Chagall from the museum of Art in Chicago.

She then selects a bright sunny day with occasional clouds to illuminate the glass. She synchronizes the time of day to match the time of the service. Then she returns to her father who is reviewing his sermon for the day.

Soon congregants start arriving at the church. Ralph and Christine greet them at the door. All of the congregants are overjoyed that Ralph has been returned to them and also greet Christine warmly.

At the appointed time, Ralph begins the service. Owing to the Anglican background of Ralph, the service has a Christian flavor and the centerpiece of the service is the sermon.

This particular sermon is special for Ralph as there was much on his mind. He felt he needed to unburden himself of all the issues that troubled him and he decided to use the sermon as a way of searching for healing, for himself, and for his congregation.

"When I was touched by God and set on this path, I had no idea where it would lead. But I knew that it would be hard. God Himself told me that it would be the hardest thing I had ever done. Those of you who have shared with me in communion have felt the aura of God's infinite love.

But nowhere in the infinitude were the words that it would be easy.

Putting this temple together, forming this religion, gathering our flock has been a constant challenge. It has cost all of us dearly. But we could do nothing else but persevere, no matter the cost.

The overriding commandment from God is love. Love God, love yourself, and love your neighbor. That's all we have to do, and yet each and every day we are challenged on those simple commandments.

We are faced with hatred daily. We see it on the street. We hear it on the news. We experience it on a personal basis.

We were attacked on a personal basis; a cowardly act of destruction and terrorism that has cost us so dearly. We have been deprived of one of our flock. And on a personal basis, I had to grieve the loss of my dearest love.

She, like the rest of us, was resurrected through technology and she sits with us today. But she has been forever changed. She will never be able to experience the joys that others her age will. She has been borne now into our world, and we welcome her with open arms and love. But she was denied the choice of entering the world of the Transcribed.

Her mother and I had to make the horrific choice of transforming her or allowing her to enter the loving arms of God. I hope that Christine will come to understand that we have made this selfish choice because we love her dearly and that she, too, has a part in the path of man on God's great journey.

And what of our attackers? What are we to make of them? How are we to respond to this horrific act? What would we say to them were they standing here with us today? How should we respond to those who hate us so much that they would kill?

I am challenged not to say that the way to answer hate is with more hate. God's challenge to me and to us is so very, very difficult. The easy path, the easiest thing, is to fall into hatred. It is a dark pit that can be hard to climb out of. I saw that personally myself when I faced God's judgment of me. It was my own hatred that judged me. It was the darkness within me that created my own personal hell.

But it was a hell with an exit. It was not eternal. But lasted only as long as I chose to hold on to my hate. When I realized I could release the darkness in me, I was welcomed into the infinite love that God promises everyone.

This love was challenged once again. And I must love. Were our attackers here with me this day, I would refuse to hate them. I would not fall down that black hole that they want me to fall in! I will not give in to hate!

And this is your challenge also. If you follow the easy path, the path that leads to hate, then you are depriving yourself of the love that God has for us all.

In the name of the Father, Son, and Holy Ghost, amen."

Ralph stepped down from the podium and approached Christine, who is sitting in the first pew. Christine and the congregation stand as he approaches her. Ralph held her hands and hugged her.

He then turned to the congregation and said, "As we are a new church, we are all of a joyful spirit when another joins our flock. So, too, I would like to welcome my daughter, Christine Allison Chalmers into our flock. While she is newly transcribed and still learning to walk around in a chassis, she has made re-markable progress.

Through counseling and training, she has chosen to have the high bandwidth link and will be joining us in communion today.

Everyone please welcome Christine in the passing of the fellowship!"

The congregation gathered around her and gave her hugs, which she felt in a more personal way than she could feel them before. Before she was transcribed, even with haptic gloves and VR helmet, Christine still felt the cold frame of the Transcribed that she touched.

But now she felt the warmth of each body in VR. Just as in the real world, she felt his or her embrace as a physical thing that every flesh and blood person felt.

Everyone came to hug her and congratulate her on joining the congregation.

Following the passing of the fellowship, the congregation returned to their alignment in preparation for communion.

Communion for the Transcribed did not depend on ceremo-ny, but preparation to engage the high bandwidth link, with Ralph as the primary focus of the data transmission.

The high bandwidth link was a combination of software modification to the computer substrate that operated the brain of the Transcribed, and hardware that allowed the higher data rates that the hack required.

The congregants used the hack, though originally, forbidden by the software vendors. Initially, the software vendors got into a patch war with the users to prevent misuse of the operating system. The congregants would bypass the patches almost as quickly as they were released.

Then the lawyers got involved. Attempting to prosecute users of the hack, the Transcribed lawyers countersued on First Amendment grounds, guaranteeing the right of free assembly, free speech, and freedom of religion. Also, anti-slavery laws were invoked because the software vendors were attempting to prevent the Transcribed from complete use of their bodies.

The software vendors finally relented when a number of the employees walked out in protest. The walkouts were by Transcribed and non-Transcribed alike.

Instead of the hack into the operating system, the vendors provided an open source interface into the software that would allow the transmission to occur.

To participate in communion, the congregation connected to each other using an optical high-speed cable that attached to the diagnostic plug. They are connected, token ring style to a device that provided coordination and arbitration of data, each person becoming a node on the ring.

The leader of the communion can then allow their sensorium to be shared with the participants. Each of the participants loses themselves into the sensorium of the leader. They feel, hear, and see everything the leader does. They also hear his thoughts, but not as someone overhears another's conversation, but actually thinks the same thoughts. They are literally thinking as one mind.

Some have called it a "hive mind". But the participation is completely voluntary and at any time individuals can remove themselves from the hive mind and continue cognition independent of the rest of the congregants. They can continue to participate on any level of communion that they choose.

Some choose to only experience the visual sensations, some only the auditory, and some the tactile feel of God.

Yet, no matter on what level they participate, they can feel the Infinite. They can feel God.

Ralph's part in communion is to use his ability as a Transcribed life to re-experience that brief instant before he was instantiated. And through overclocking, they can slow down that instant and feel the depth of love that is God.

There is no sensorium recollection of Ralph's time with God. The only thing Ralph remembers of that time is flashes and images. But the last instant is clear. Like the echo of a tolling bell, they can still feel the echo of God, truth and faith together.

And through that sharing, they become one.

Christine had previously installed the high bandwidth hack but this was the first time, other than diagnostic testing, that she had an actual chance to use it.

She communed with her father on a level that she had never known. In that brief instant of time, not only did she touch the face of God, but figuratively turned to touch her father, and there came to know the deep and abiding love he held for her.

On the day of her return, Emily and David waited anxiously. Christine had not been back to the house since the day of the attack, less than a week before. Emily visited her once in FIVR; Dave visited a few times in VR. To Christine's time sense however, she had been gone more than a month. In addition to VR rehab and training in using her new chassis, she had also received counseling to help her through the terrible experience she had. That counseling would continue for many more weeks, both in real time with her parents and in overclock with her counselor and in group therapy.

All of the family members had gone to grief counseling, even though Christine survived the attack. Christine had effectively been horribly mutilated and could only survive inside a box. Emily's dreams for her daughter had been shattered. David, too, had experienced a loss. Forced to choose between his church and his family, he had not only felt the loss of a child, but had had his religious conviction severely challenged. He felt lost and adrift.

The house announced the arrival of Ralph and Christine. Dave told the house to let them enter, and in rolled two chassis. On one screen is the visage of Ralph and on the other is Christine.

This is the first time that Emily had seen Christine in a chassis and she is dumbstruck. *Oh my God! What have I done?* she thought, as she tried to put on a good face.

"Christine! Honey!" Christine rolled over to her mother and automatically reached out to hug her. Emily unconsciously pulled back.

"Mom? What's wrong? I'm still me! I want to hold you!"

Emily pulled herself together and reached for her daughter.

"Honey, it's all right. I was just surprised, that's all."

They embraced, mother to daughter, machine to flesh.

"I wish I could kiss you," said Emily.

"You could, but it would smear my screen," giggled Christine.

They pulled back but held each other's hands.

"You seem to have taken very well to your chassis. I like your color scheme." It was possible to change the color and pattern of the chassis and torso through the use of an active nano based paint. Christine had chosen a subtle pale blue as the base color and metal flaked daisies to decorate the chassis. Her torso was a flesh tone of her previous body and had a tee shirt and skirt drawn over that. Even though she had a mechanical body, she felt slightly embarrassed to go out "naked".

"Don't say that, Mom. You make be feel like a new car."

"Honey, no, I didn't mean it like…"

"It's all right, Mom, that's what Dad said, too. I haven't settled on any particular color or pattern, I like to make it up. After all, effectively I'm going around without any clothes on, so I might as well be flashy."

"There is that, dear, but if you like I'm sure we could print up a dress that could fit you," said Emily, getting into the humor of the moment.

"Nah, I think the skirt would just get tangled up in my treads."

Dave said, "We were just going to have supper."

"Go right ahead, Dave," said Christine. "I'm not hungry. I topped off my cells before we left."

"Is that how you…?"

"Yeah, we plug in when we feel hungry. We can deploy our solar collectors too, but it takes longer."

Ralph was feeling awkward and felt it would be better if he left so Chris could try to get back in the swing of her new life.

"Well, I'm going to go. Chris is there anything you need?"

"No, Dad, I'm fine."

"Ok, call me if you have any questions. Your chassis AI can help you with most issues and you can also call the chassis help line if there are any other questions."

"Will do, Dad." Ralph and Chris hugged; they don't kiss. Ralph headed for the door.

"Christine how does it feel?" asked Dave.

"How does what feel?"

Gesturing to the chassis, "That. Being inside the machine. Do you feel it?"

"No, really it hardly feels any different at all. I feel the same way I always did. It's a little more work to remember where my chassis is, because I'm wider now, but it all just feels normal now. I walk and talk the same way I used to. It was supposed to be that way."

"Do you remember anything about the explosion?" Dave asked innocently.

"Dave! Please! It was hard enough. It's barely been a week since all this happened. Don't bring this up. It's upsetting," scolded Emily.

"I'm sorry, Em." Turning to Christine, he said, "I didn't mean anything by it, Chris."

"It's Ok, Dave. I've had a few weeks of counseling and I've muted the memories so they don't feel so raw."

"A few weeks?"

"It's overclocking Dave. We talked about that," said Emily.

"I figured that you were running faster, but I didn't really think how much faster. How much time has passed for you, Chris?"

"It feels like about a month. I've spent most of it in overclock. My therapist recommended that I turn the emotions down on that experience until I can put more perspective on it."

"We're still working through it as well. We've been seeing a grief counselor, too."

"I'm over the worst of it now. I've pretty much come to accept what's happened and just want to go on."

"You said you could turn the emotions down on your memories."

"Yes, I can do that now. Just about every memory is a combination of things. Most people remember the visual, but there are other things as well. Memories cause emotions, and intense memories cause intense emotions. I can tag those memories and turn them down so that when I remember them, they don't cause an emotional overload."

"That is helpful, I guess."

"Some, yes, but I can't quit thinking of poor Dale. He was the nicest man."

"He triggered the explosion, didn't he?"

"We don't know what triggered it. The police are still looking into it. They haven't made their final report yet."

"I'll never forgive myself for letting you stay with your father that extra day. If I had insisted you come back none of this would have happened," said Emily.

"The bomb would still have happened, Mom. If I hadn't been there it might have been Dad who was killed."

Dave mumbled something under his breath.

"He didn't die in the accident!" yelled Christine.

"I didn't say anything!" said Dave.

"I heard you. I can hear a lot more than I used to, and you whispered that Daddy died years ago in the car accident!"

"Christine! I won't let you say such things about Dave. I didn't hear him say anything. You apologize this instant!"

"I won't. You want me to play it back with amplification, Dave? You've always hated my father!"

"I don't have to put up with this." Dave stormed out of the room.

"Dave!" Emily turned on Christine furiously. "Christine! See what you've done? You've just come back and already you're causing strife. There was no need to accuse him."

"I didn't accuse him. I heard him plain as day. This is all about Pastor Tim isn't it? I heard he wanted me to die, that he wanted you to pull the plug on me. He thinks I'm evil because I have a computer for a brain."

"Christine, you go and apologize right now to Dave! I'll have you know that when Pastor Tim demanded that we pull the plug because he said God would send you to Hell, Dave told him to leave. He said that the church would not come between him and HIS family. That includes YOU! He kicked the pastor out. He came to your defense. You should be ashamed! We've left his church because of this, even though he's known Tim most of his life. He loves you no matter what."

Emily could not bring herself to tell Christine that she had given serious consideration to pulling the plug on the transcription, which would have killed Christine. She still felt horrible about herself to even think it. It had been Dave that talked her out of it.

"Mom, I'm so sorry. I didn't know. I feel terrible."

"I thought you could dial your emotions down," she said sarcastically.

"They auto adjust and right now I think I should let them."

Christine begins to sob. "I didn't know." Christine tries to put her head in her hands but is stopped by the screen that now serves as her head.

"I don't have tears anymore, but I still cry."

Emily gets up and puts her arms around her daughter. Christine hugs her mother. Flesh to metal, but the affection is still the same.

Christine continues to sob and Emily holds her as she always did. Emily thinks to herself, *Not that much has changed. She's still my little girl.*

After some moments, Christine finishes her sobbing and looks up at her mother.

"Thank you, Mom."

"For what?"

"For holding me. I didn't think you ever would. I can feel it you know."

"I can feel it too, Honey. Now go and apologize to Dave. I'll go with you if you want."

"No, I'll go, it's all right."

Christine left the room and Emily sat down. She sobbed a little bit, too.

Christine goes into the den where Dave is watching something on the big screen.

"Dave."

"Yes, Chris?"

"I want to apologize. What I said was wrong. I heard what you told Pastor Tim. It was wrong of me to say such a hurtful thing."

"Chris, thank you. I appreciate it. The pastor has gotten very extreme lately. He wasn't always that way. He was upsetting your mother and we were still trying to come to grips with everything that happened. And he goes off like that. It wasn't right. Chris, understand that this is all new to me, too. I've known about the Transcribed, of course, but I never expected all of this to be so close. Your father and mother still have issues about what happened to him and sometimes I pick up on it. It was never meant to make you feel bad. I still don't know what to make of all this, I feel blindsided."

"I was never expecting it either."

"Well, now that you're here. Do you need anything special?"

"For what?"

"For your chassis, for you. I don't know if you need a bed or if you need any special support equipment or wiring, I've been caught a little flat-footed in this."

"No, I'm fine. My chassis will recharge by plugging into a power outlet. I don't need a bed or even chairs anymore. I don't sleep, but I do need some time to relax. My brain still acts like a flesh and blood brain, and people sleep so the body can rebuild and the brain can organize its memories. I still need to do that, but I don't need sleep to do it. I just have to sit quietly for a while."

"No chairs?"

"The chassis is my chair, my throne, my chariot. I don't feel the need to ever sit now."

"That's interesting. I never knew that. It never occurred to me."

"I would have never have thought of it either."

"So do you want me to take your bed out of your room?"

"Yes, please, it'll give me a little more room to move around."

"Ok, I'll take care of it tomorrow. What about school?"

"What about it?"

"I guess we have to get you re-enrolled."

"You don't really have to Dave. I can download anything I need to know."

"But school is more than just learning things. It's interaction with other students, it's learning to grow up."

Gesturing at her body Christine said, "How am I going to interact with other students like this? I'm not like other kids anymore."

"No, you're not. Not anymore."

"Besides, I can take lessons in VR and also interact with other kids like me there, too."

"Chris, there's a difference between knowledge and wisdom. Just being able to download an answer to a question does not make you wise."

"I know. I have to talk with other kids."

"You have to interact with society, Hon, you can't spend your life in VR."

"There are some that say there is nothing the real world has that they want."

"I hope you aren't one of them."

"No, but you have to admit, VR can have everything you can do in the real world."

"Except God. God is not in VR."

"That isn't true. I've been to communion. I've experienced Dad's memory. He truly did see God, I know it."

"Chris, this is what Pastor Tim was talking about. God doesn't exist in VR. What your father experienced was a software malfunction. A glitch. He was so badly injured in the crash his brain was damaged. It was a miracle that he survived the transcription."

"You said it was a miracle. So doesn't that show that God was involved? If it was, then why couldn't Daddy see God?"

"Chris, that isn't what I meant. I just meant that he was incredibly lucky but..."

Emily, hearing the conversation comes into the room.

"Chris," said Emily, "What are you talking about?"

"Dave is saying that Dad hallucinated and his memories aren't real."

"You mean about the pre-boot memories that he's based his religion on?"

"Yes"

"You've seen them?"

"Yes, and it's true! I've felt it! I felt exactly what he felt and it's all true. There is a God and He is love!"

"Chris, he tried to show that stuff to me and it was just gibberish. All I saw was lights and colors, there wasn't anything there."

"Mom, you're wrong. I don't know why you couldn't see it, but I did and I can't deny what I saw and felt."

"Chris, this is just wrong. I've put up with your father and that heathen trash he does, but I swear he's just a charlatan. I forbid you to ever set foot in that place again! Your father has visitation, but I can sue to prevent him from infecting you with these heretical ideas. You're endangering your soul by playing with fire. God will punish you!"

"So you believe what Tim was saying? You should have killed me?"

"How dare you! You are my daughter! Don't you ever say that again! Dammit, I love you! I…" Emily broke down weeping and rushed from the room.

"Christine, you are so hateful!" and Dave went after Emily.

"You all just think I'm a robot! A talking computer! What do you want from me? Do you want me to do your taxes? Or maybe I can be your search engine!"

Emily charged back in the room furiously.

"Mom, I've downloaded the Bible and all its variations, including the NIV, New American Standard, King James, New King James and sixteen others. I've also learned both Aramaic and Greek to read them in their original languages. I've also downloaded the Qua-ran, and Talmud. According to all of those, it was Tim who was the false prophet by preaching hate, not love."

"That's it! I'm suing your father for complete custody! He's turned you against us! He's filled your head with these absurd ideas and he's trying to get you to turn your back on God! You're coming back here to stay and we'll find a church that will help you to see that there is only one true way! And it's not his! He has turned to Satan as his god and he's trying to take you to hell with him!"

"You can't do that!"

"Yes I can! I'm your mother and you are under the age of consent! Once I get a judgment against him I'll be able to send you to a school that will take these ideas out of your head and show you the truth of the Bible."

"Which one?" Christine countered.

"What do you mean?" asked Emily.

"Which of the sixteen current translations of the Bible do you mean? The one where Adam and Eve ate the apple, or the one where they fell into sin by having sex? Or perhaps the Aramaic version? And what about the parts they left out?"

"Don't talk nonsense to me. I don't care how many Bibles you've read, you are no scholar. Now, go to your room!"

"You're done playing with your computer and now you're telling it to put itself away?"

"Get out!" yelled Emily.

Christine rolls out of the den and heads upstairs to her room. Sending Christine to her room was not the punishment Emily had in mind. She still had full access to the net and could even visit VR. She called her father.

"Daddy! Mom's going to take me away from you!"

"What? What happened? What brought this on?"

"We had a fight and she says you're filling my head with lies because I went to communion. She thinks I've been taken over by the devil or something."

"Your mother has had some pretty extreme ideas ever since she started dating Dave and going to that crazy ass church."

"They've left Pastor Tim, but are looking for another place to go and they want to send me to a school where I'll get proper Bible training."

"All right, this has gone too far. You aren't old enough yet to be able to divorce your parents or choose whom you stay with. I'll talk to my lawyer again and see what we can do."

"I don't want to leave you, Daddy!"

"You won't."

"Mom thinks she can take me away any time she wants."

"I think that she has more to learn about the law. I think she'll find out soon enough. I never wanted this to happen. We parted amicably enough, but this is just crazy."

"Can she take me away?"

"No, not legally. I'm your father and I have rights as well. The last time I talked with the lawyer which was just before the attack, he said that I had a number of points to make that would make it difficult for your mother to change the visitation, let alone take custody."

"I want to live with you. I've always been bored here. And now that I'm Transcribed, I can really understand the others in the church. I want to be part of the church, your church. I want to become a minister!"

"Hon, let's take this one step at a time. I'll call my lawyer and see what can be done. These custody battles always get ugly, but I'll make sure you are taken care of."

"What about becoming a minister?"

"Hon, you've only been to one communion. There's really more to it than that. Of course I would love to have you involved with the church. But, you're just ten years old. That's a little young, even for Transcribed people. I'll try to come up with things you can read and learn. Of course you can continue being an acolyte, and we'll see where it goes. We'll talk more when you come to visit."

"I hope so. Mom seems to think she can do all that stuff now."

"Trust me, it will take much longer than that. She has to go to court and show cause then we get to respond. It could go back and forth for months. It'll be fine, don't worry."

"Are you sure?"

"Yes, Hon, really.

"What should I do in the meantime?"

"Nothing right now. Let me call the lawyer and see what we can do. Please do not run away. If you do, it could make it more difficult for us to make our case for you. If your mother does anything that you think will make your life more difficult, call me. If I have to, I'll call the police."

"Ok, Dad. But please hurry, I don't know that I can take this for a long time."

"No worries, Hon. You have access to VR so we can meet in person anytime."

"Yes, but that's not the real world."

"I know Hon, just try to remain calm. You can do that you know. Just dial the anxiety down and try to try not to provoke your mother or Dave."

"I'll try, Dad."

"Ok, I'll be in touch. Talk to you soon."

The service at The First Baptist Church is a very different experience than that at The First Church of the Transcribed. They take a literal approach to the Bible and view it as an actual historical document of God's participation in the world and demonstration of his guiding hand in man's journey to ascendancy. The church concentrates on the Old Testament to show man's fallibility and how only God can provide guidance.

Reverend Misinger conducts the service in a rather strict way. There is a choir and communion is only held on the first of the month.

Reverend Misinger is a tall man who believes in strict adherence to the Bible as the actual word of God. Drawing from various aspects of other Baptist denominations, and as dictated in the Old Testament, it forbids women from having any pastoral place in the church or its service.

It had been one week since the explosion at the Transcribed church and Tim was especially dour as he approached the pulpit. Dave and Emily were no longer welcomed in the church and did not attend.

When he took to the pulpit he looked out at his congregation and spoke.

"You may have seen on the news of the incident that happened recently where a robot was destroyed in an accident. The details from the media say that it may have been a bomb yet there are questions that remain unresolved. There was some additional damage as well.

Nevertheless, the salient fact is that an infernal machine of Satan was sent back to the pits of Hell where it belongs. And for that we should be grateful. We cannot condone violence yet we cannot turn away when the good work of righteous God has been done.

God is righteous and vengeful! He has repeatedly shown man the errors of his ways by striking down the wicked as He did in Sodom and Gomorrah.

God became angry with Eve when she bit the apple that Satan, in the guise of a serpent, used to beguile her. For her transgressions God evicted both Adam and Eve from the idyllic place of Eden. He leveled Tyre for speaking against Jerusalem.

Do we need further proof of God's might? And yet man continues to mock God in every way. We should be fearful of His wrath. We need to heed the obvious innumerable signs He has given us.

God's grace does not extend to machines. We cannot save them for they have no souls. That which they claim to be, died, and their bodies were horribly defiled. Their souls ripped from their bodies. Their brains put through a meat grinder and their bodies destroyed by horrible nano-machines.

You cannot take the soul out of a man and put it in a machine.

We must fight against this rising tide before they come for you and force you to die at their hands. We must continue to resist recognition of the idiotic term, "Machine Intelligence". There are no intelligent machines.

We have no reason to fear machines, nor do we fear technology. Machines and technology have served man since the first days we were put upon this earth. But it is just that. Technology has served man, not the other way around.

You have self-driving cars and houses that speak; yet they do not live. They cannot think and they cannot have souls. You have instantaneous communication with anyone on the planet, yet your phone has no soul and cannot ascend to Heaven.

It is the soul that God gives us that sets us apart from the beasts. God has given each and every one of you a soul. This is what should be cherished, not the tools of man. Machines are just tools to be used. We must take our world back from these machines that are forcing us to serve them. We must resist any further infringement on our lives by Satan and his infernal demons on treads.

What shall it be then? Do you not see them on the street? Pretending to be one of us? These walking, talking computers that try to fool us into Satan's evil grasp?

They beguile us; they speak like the serpent of the garden. They try to woo us away from God through their silver tongue. Like Eve we are beguiled and look to them for a connection to ones who have already passed.

But know this, my brothers! They are evil incarnate! The wonders of technology extend like the tower of Babel trying to climb to heaven. We have lost our control of the things we have created. Like Ezekiel, we worship at the image of the beast. Machines were made by man to serve man, and man was given dominion over all the earth. Man does not serve machine! Man serves God! Yet today man must serve machine as they walk among us pretending to be the loved ones whose souls are in heaven. We are told that we must obey them as if they are human beings! They are accorded all the rights of the flesh and blood. But they cannot have the body of Christ. They cannot ever become one with the Lord. They are like the golden calf. They are a false idol. And God will strike down man because he thinks to become greater than God!

We are building a new tower of Babel. We will bring the wrath of God down upon this earth for spitting in his face to allow these abominations to continue to walk among us.

Whom shall you serve, God or machine?"

The service ended soon after and Reverend Tim stood at the exit and spoke to each parishioner as they left the church.

When the congregants had departed, Tim returned to his office in the church. There he met with others who shared his hatred for the Transcribed. Among these men, one of whom is a significant contributor to the church, is William Tassant.

Tim sat down behind his desk and looked at William. "Bill, what happened? You were supposed to wait until they took the box into the church."

"We still don't know. It was rigged to go off when they opened it, but it went off early. But we got one of them anyway."

"You fool, you killed a child! That priest's daughter was there and she was right in front of the bomb! She was hit with the shrapnel of the bomb and the robot you destroyed! And on top of that, her mother agreed to have her Transcribed! The numbers are the same! Nothing changed except that we're all murderers in the eyes of God! What have you done?"

"Listen no one was supposed to get hurt! She was supposed to be in church when the bomb went off. You told them to bring her here. We were just going to turn off a bunch of robots that's all. And listen, Tim, you're in this just as deep as we are. If anyone turns on us, we all go down. So right now we have to keep this quiet."

"Well, we had best finish the job. I've excommunicated Dave and Emily from the church for what they've done. They've brought this on themselves. This time we have to make sure that those robots are destroyed and they're memories aren't used against us. If we don't send a clear message that robots aren't people, they'll have us all killed and put into those boxes."

"Well, we can't use a bomb again, they'd be wise to that."

"No, I think we have to take a more personal approach."

CHAPTER 8

After tumultuous weeks of complaints between Ralph and Emily over parenting rights, Christine returns to the Church, and Ralph.

After some heated phone calls, the lawyers got involved. Ralph's lawyer sent a letter to Family Court asking for an immediate hearing regarding the recuperation of Christine. Ralph maintained that he was better suited to help Christine recover from her transcription and provide training so that she can better learn how to use her chassis.

Emily, through her lawyer, countered that Ralph was an unfit parent. Since Christine nearly lost her life being at the church, it fell to reason that Ralph would continue to endanger Christine while there.

At a minimum, they said, Ralph should not be allowed to have Christine at the church and all visitations should be supervised.

The judge called in an advocate, who was not Transcribed, for Christine who would evaluate the situation and make a recommendation to the court based exclusively on Christine's well being.

The advocate interviewed Christine. And in order to do it properly she interviewed her in FIVR. She wanted to get her most "human" feelings and decide what the issues were in the case.

They met in a FIVR environment, which was an outdoor environment, where they shared tea.

"Christine, how have you been?"

"I'm really fine. I have been through some terrible stuff lately, but I'm coping, I guess."

"Why do you say 'I guess'?"

"No reason, I can't change back, so I have to deal with what I am now."

"That is a very mature statement. Not all adults feel that way, I wish they would."

"I've had a lot of counseling."

"But you've only been transcribed a few weeks."

"Much of it has been overclocked. To me it feels like it's been about six months."

"I've heard about overclocking but I didn't think it was quite like that."

"I'm in group therapy with other Transcribed that ended up here through accident or murder."

"Are there many murdered victims?"

"No, just a few. But it does change their outlook."

"I would think so. But let's talk about you, Christine. I'm here to speak on your behalf. What are you feeling?"

"My Mom just wants me to stay with her and go to her church. She thinks my Dad is crazy and shouldn't be around me."

"How do you feel about that? Do you think your father is insane?"

"No! I've seen his memories; I've been to communion. I know it's all true! I want to be with him."

"But what about your mother?"

"I don't want to lose her either, but I can't be wrapped up in a box. I don't want to be smothered."

"Well given what's happened, don't you think that she has a point?"

"I can understand why she thinks that way, but I don't want to be locked up!"

"Do you think your father had any involvement with the bomb or the incident?"

"No, of course not! Why would you think such a thing?"

"I'm sorry, but I have to examine all sides to the matter so I can be a proper representative for you. I have your interests uppermost in my mind. I speak only for you."

"Ok."

"Do you think that your father does anything to stir up trouble with anyone?"

"No! All we want to do is have our church. My father talks to other Transcribed or their families. He has counseled a lot of people."

"So you would prefer to go with your father?"

"Yes, I've said that. I need to learn more about being Transcribed. He can teach me. Also, I want to keep going to his church. I'm an acolyte there and I do designs on the cathedral. The others there like me and I miss them. I have so much to learn from them."

"Ok, Christine, I understand. I've reviewed the issues and I will recommend to the judge that you continue to be with your father."

"Does that mean I can go back to him?"

"That actually is for the judge to decide. But your voice, through me, will be as important as what your Mother and Father say. More so, actually as this is all about you and your well being."

At the family court hearing, both sides plus Christine, through her advocate, made their case.

Emily wanted sole custody claiming that Ralph had endangered Christine and as a result of his reckless endangerment had caused grievous harm to Christine so severely that she had to be transcribed to save any part of her life.

Ralph countered that as her father, he was entitled to continued visitation with Christine and was an upstanding member of the community, and could continue to teach her about her new life as Transcribed. The incident that caused her transcription was unforeseen and he was not the cause of the bomb.

Christine's advocate, after reviewing the case and interviewing Christine, found her well adjusted to her condition. She still held her father in high regard and felt that he could help teach her and help her to adjust to her new life.

After deliberation, the judge found that while Christine was severely injured as a result of the blast, that was no reason to prevent her from continued visitation with her father. Moreover, for a period of time not to extend more than three wall-clock months, Christine could have visitation every week. This increased visitation would be to help her adjust to her new life. Additionally, Ralph and his environment for Christine, both virtual and real, would be under scrutiny to ensure a good environment for Christine. The judge would receive regular updates from the advocate. Christine could continue her schooling in VR without having to attend school in real space.

Emily was furious at the judgment and vowed to appeal her case. But in the meantime, would abide by the judge's ruling.

The following Friday, Ralph went to pick Christine up from her mother's house. When Ralph came to the door, he found that the security system no longer recognized him and he had to wait until Emily opened the door for him.

She didn't let Ralph in; rather she came out on the porch and closed the door behind her.

"Is Christine ready?" Dave asked.

"She'll be out in a minute. I want you to know that just because you won this round that you have not in any way changed my mind about taking Chris. She belongs with me. You should be tried for murder! You murdered my daughter!"

Ralph took a 'virtual' deep breath and dialed his emotions down.

"Em, this is ridiculous! How can you say that! I had nothing to do with that bomb! I never intended to see her hurt. I love Chris."

"All I have of her is this machine. You've taken her away from me and you're trying to poison her mind with all this communion with God crap."

"Em, I won't get into this with you. Bring Christine out now."

"I still don't think it's a good idea. She should stay with me."

"Em, if you don't bring her out now, I will call the police and make a report that you are trying to deny me access to my daughter. Do you want that kind of scene? Do you want this reported to the court? I've been very gracious in all this, and I could easily make a case to take custody, too. Do you want that? Do you?"

Emily just stared at his face on the screen and then went into the house without another word and slammed the door behind her.

After a few minutes Christine came out. Her face was grim. But brightened when she saw her father.

"Daddy!" She leaned over and hugged him. It was awkward in their chassis but it was heartfelt.

"Oh, I'm so glad you're here. This week has been a nightmare. Mom has been doing nothing but ranting on how you are devil spawn or something. I kept my emotions dialed down like you asked and didn't provoke her, but it didn't make it any easier."

"I know, Hon. I'm so sorry you have to go through this. Let's get going."

They both entered Ralph's car and headed back to the church. Along the way Christine talked more about how Emily was becoming more outraged by the situation.

Christine still felt awkward about moving around in her chassis, even though she has spent several days in overclocking sim and many hours in real time in her actual chassis.

"Dad, this still feels weird. I feel like I'm walking and when I look down I can see my legs overlaid on the chassis, but it still feels a bit like I'm floating. Climbing stairs is very strange. I can feel my tread touch the stair, and I feel myself walking up the stairs, but I still feel like I'm floating."

"Yes, it is that way. You'll get used to it over time."

"I'm not really human anymore, am I?"

"Why on earth would you say that, Christine?"

"It's just so different, so strange."

"Wouldn't you feel that way if you had to live in a wheel chair? Your life would be drastically changed, but you'd still be human."

"Yes, I know, the crisis counselor said the same thing. The sims and training helped me learn how to use a chassis, but now that I'm in the real world, it strikes me how very different I've become."

"Yes, it is. But it's not a handicap. In many ways it's an improvement. We can know more things, more easily, and it is knowledge, not just information. When you download information, it integrates with your cerebral cortex. It's more than doing a simple search, and getting a bunch of results. It's actual learning! It is incredible! You don't have to return to school to be taught, you can *learn* simply by wishing it."

"Well, Dad, school is more than just the classes. Part of it was going to see my friends and meeting with them and stuff."

"You can still meet with your friends, Chris. I'd be happy to have them come over, or you could go see them."

"No, Dad, I'm still a bit embarrassed about how I look."

"What do you mean?"

"To them, I look like a robot! They'd make fun of me behind my back or treat me like a cripple."

"Then they weren't really your friends, Hon. Also Honey, we don't really use the term robot. It's pejorative. It denies who we are. We are still human beings, we are still people."

"Well, it's what they would think."

"Then you have to try to change their minds."

"Why me? Why should I have to do it? I never asked to be this way!"

"Few of us do, honey. But we can't run away from who we are, and the only way to change people's minds is to be among them. Have them see that we are no different, really, than who we started out as. We've been through a horrible life changing event, but we have to show them that it hasn't changed us."

"I never asked to become a spokesman for a whole people. It's scary."

"I know, but you are strong enough for it."

"That may be, but I'm not up for seeing any of them yet."

"That's OK. Say, do you want to see some of the benefits of being Transcribed?"

"No more downloads, Dad, I've had my fill."

"No, something more fun!"

"OK, what?"

"You'll see. Come along."

They left the church and went outside. Ralph led the way, though Christine still felt a little embarrassed and unprotected going out into the world as Transcribed.

"There's a carnival in the area and there's something I want you to try."

"What? A ride for the Transcribed?"

"No, you'll see."

They rolled through the late afternoon sun down a few blocks to one of the nearby neighborhoods. As they got closer to the carnival, they passed by people, some of whom eye them suspiciously. Seeing a Transcribed in the flesh, as it were, was still somewhat of an oddity.

They arrived at the carnival just as night was falling. Ralph and Christine rolled by the various rides and barkers' tents and go to the back of the carnival area. There they find batting cages and other amusements.

"Is this what you wanted to show me?" asks Christine.

"Yes, that one at the end is vacant, go on in."

As they were about to enter the attendant comes up to them.

"Excuse me, but you have to wear a helmet."

"What?" asked Ralph incredulously.

"I'm sorry, but our insurance is quite specific. Anyone going into the batting cages must wear a helmet."

"You realize how ridiculous that is? Even if one of those balls did hit me, it would just bounce off! Also, my brain isn't in my head, it's in an armored box inside my chassis."

"Sorry, no helmet, no entry." The attendant handed helmets to Ralph and Christine.

"I don't think it will fit, Dad."

"Do we have to wear them on our heads?"

"That's where most people put them," the attendant replied sarcastically.

"Yes, but do we have to?"

"I don't care where you put them, just as long as they're on your body."

"Ok, thanks."

Ralph and Christine went into the cage. Ralph leaned down and affixed the helmet at the bottom of Christine's torso on top of the small deck of her tread unit. The attendant looked at them disgustedly.

Looking back at the attendant Ralph said, "Well, that's where her brain really is."

Ralph spun around and located his helmet in a similar fashion.

Ralph picked up a bat and handed it to Christine.

"Ok, now take a few swings and I'll trigger a ball. I'll set it for a slow pitch."

Christine took a few experimental swings with the bat and looked over to her father and nodded for him to trigger the release. Ralph triggered the ball and it arced slowly toward Christine. Christine swung and missed the ball by a wide margin.

"I've never been very good at this, Dad."

"It's all right, Hon, just keep your eye on the ball. Here comes another one."

Ralph triggered another ball and while Christine tipped the ball, it still got past her.

"Ok, hon, now go into overclock mode and try again."

Christine looked at her father and nodded. As soon as she nodded, Christine flipped into overclock mode, and while her servomotors were still the same speed, her reaction time was greatly improved. It seemed to take several seconds for her head to spin back to the pitching machine and her arms to get into position. It seemed to take a long time for the machine to throw the ball. The ball seemed to lazily make its way to Christine. She had plenty of time to take aim and swing the bat and she connected with it easily. The ball jumped off her bat and started to arc away from her. Christine dropped back into normal mode and watched the ball streak away in real time.

Turning to her father she said, "That was incredible! The ball just seemed to float toward me. I had plenty of time to line up my swing!"

"Want to try some more?"

"Sure!"

"Ok, I'm going to set it to random mode. It'll continuously shoot balls at various speeds and spins."

Christine easily hit each ball as it was pitched. Then as she gained confidence, she started to hit them harder and harder. The balls seem to explode off her bat and hit the back of the batting cage with more and more force.

"Hey! Robots! Quit trying to show off!"

Ralph stopped the pitching machine and both he and Christine turned to see that a group of people had gathered around the cage. They looked hostile.

"Excuse me, what did you say?" said Ralph to the crowd.

A man stepped forward to the front of the cage. "You heard me, robot! You've got super-hearing."

"That was completely uncalled for. We are not robots! My daughter and I are just as human as you are," replied Ralph as he rolled to confront the man.

"You're nothing but a bunch of wires and shit pretending to be someone who died. Now get the fuck out before we disassemble you!"

Ralph dialed back his emotions and prepared to trigger an emergency alarm if the confrontation turned ugly.

"We'll do no such thing. We have a right to be here and we won't be bullied by the likes of you!"

"I said get the fuck out or we'll make you leave!"

"Do you want to try?" said Ralph aggressively.

"Dad, let's just leave. We don't need this nonsense." Christine said as she rolled up next to her father.

"No, Chris, this is what we are fighting for. We are human; we've always been human. And this dolt is as ignorant as someone making fun of a person in a wheelchair."

"You're not human! You're a fucking computer! This place is for flesh and blood people, not fucking machines!" The crowd started yelling more invectives emboldened by the rabble-rouser. Someone threw a bottle over the top of the cage, which just missed both Ralph and Christine.

Ralph whispered, "Chris, in your visual menu, open up the panel that says Emergency. Click the one marked Police. Tell them what is happening."

Ralph turned to the crowd. "We've called the police and they are on their way. Leave now or we'll press charges."

Christine contacted the police and told them of the potential riot.

"I'm not afraid of you! You're just a vacuum cleaner, a fucking toaster!"

One of the police on patrol at the carnival pushed his way into the crowd. He pushed himself in front of the man doing all the yelling.

"What's going on here?" asked the officer.

"These robots don't belong here!"

The policeman got right in the man's face. "First of all, you will dial it down or I'll take you in. Second, the law says these people are human, and they have a right to be here. So if you don't want to spend the night in jail, you'll leave now. I've called for backup and we'll take the lot of you in."

"It's a fucking stupid law!"

"I don't get paid to decide what law is stupid. Now leave!"

In the distance sirens could be heard. Some of the crowd moved off. But the man is livid.

"Fucking toasters!" With that he tried to push his way around the policeman and lunge at the cage.

"Ok, that's it." With that the policeman grabbed the man and put him in an arm lock and pushed his body against the cage. He handcuffed the man, spun him around, and pushed his back against the cage.

"You're going in."

"What the fuck for? I didn't do anything!"

"Shut up now or there'll be more charges. You are going in for disorderly conduct and assaulting a policeman."

A police van rolled up and two more policemen got out. They started to break up the crowd. The crowd moved off slowly.

The policeman took the man to the back of the van and put him in. After speaking briefly to the two other officers, he came up to the cage where Ralph and Christine were still standing.

"Ok, what happened here?" he asked.

"I was showing my daughter how to hit baseballs. I used to be on a softball team. She was really enjoying herself. Then that idiot started yelling at us."

"Did he attack or physically assault you?"

"No, he was just being a loudmouth, but it was starting to turn ugly."

"I'm going to take him in since he assaulted me. But did you want to press any charges?"

"No, he was just being ignorant. Maybe he should learn some manners. I don't think that there's anything you could charge him with anyway. Being ignorant isn't against the law," said Ralph.

"Let me get your names and information for the report." Ralph and Christine gave the officer their information.

"I'm going to take this one in. But there'll be a couple of officers on patrol if you want to stay."

Christine turned to the officer. "No, they've pretty much ruined the night for me. Let's go home, Dad."

"Ok, Chris. But if we leave, the bullies win."

"Daddy, I'm not here to make a statement. I was just trying to enjoy myself."

"I understand, Honey. Let's go home."

Ralph and Christine left the batting cage. The officer turned to watch them leave.

"I'm sorry this happened," he said. "Please be careful on your way home."

Ralph turned to the officer. "Thank you, Sir. We will."

As they rolled through the night air, Ralph said, "I was going to tell you that there is also a targeting app that you can use on your visual field that can help you hit the ball, too, but you were doing pretty well on your own."

"I suppose I could do something similar with pitching, too. " said Christine.

"Yeah, though you'd need more practice getting your pitch to do what you want, but you could throw ninety miles an hour balls all day."

"So we'd really clean up at the pitching booths at the carnival, then too, huh?"

"Yeah, they don't allow me to play. They say I have an unfair advantage."

"We do, don't we?" asked Christine.

"Yes, that is one of the things I was trying to show you. We're not invalids, we aren't handicapped. We're enhanced!"

"People hate us because we're better than them?"

"No, honey, we're not better, never think that. All people are the same. We're no longer bound by the limitations of the flesh and blood human body. But that doesn't make us better. We're still the same people even without the enhancements."

"I wish those haters understood that, too."

"It takes time, Honey, but it will change in time. I have faith."

"I hope so, Dad. But time seems to move so slowly sometimes."

"You want to see something else you can do now?"

"Sure, what's that?"

"Follow me."

Ralph headed into an empty field away from the carnival and most of the lights. He stopped in the middle of the field.

"What are we doing here?" asked Christine.

"Look up at the stars, Chris. Look at the moon."

She looked up. "Now what?"

"Change your clocking value to minus one point five."

"Underclocking?" she asked.

"Yes, do that and now watch the moon. Don't talk until I speak to you. Your voice will be slowed down as well and I won't be able to understand you until I clock down as well."

Christine looked up at the moon and underclocked her computer.

"It's speeding across the sky! I can see it move!"

After what seemed like minutes, Ralph finally spoke.

"What was that? I didn't catch that first part. I was still spinning down."

"Daddy! The moon, it's racing across the sky! I can see the stars move!"

"Wonderful isn't it? That is one of the wonders of our new life. We don't really have to be slaves to the same clock as everyone else. You can speed up to watch a hummingbird's wings or slow down and watch the stars speed across the sky."

"I never thought it would be this beautiful!"

"The world can be a wonderful place if you want it to be."

"Thank you, Daddy."

"I love you, Chris. Let's just sit and watch the moon set."

The two of them watched the moon for hours, not speaking, barely moving, as their underclocked computers took in the wonders of the Universe.

After the moon set, Ralph and Christine started rolling home. It was late, not that they cared. They could remain awake indefinitely, and only needed some quiet time to organize their thoughts. They would normally stay up to all hours, but this was one of the few times that they were out and about late.

As they rolled down the deserted street, they crossed an alleyway, and they both came up short.

"Did you hear that?"

"Yes I did, Hon, can you tell what it is?"

"It sounds like a kitten. It sounds hurt. I want to check it out."

"Hold on a second, Christine, let me go first. I'll look in the range of IR that I have." Ralph scanned the area and pinpointed the source of the sound.

"It seems to be coming from behind those boxes."

Christine rolled up. Ralph picked up a bundle of fur, mewling at the top of its lungs. The reason was obvious.

"How could someone be so cruel? Why would they bind its legs to its body like that?"

"There are some sick people in the world, Hon. Let's be glad this is all they did. It looks fine except for the binding."

Someone had taped the kitten's legs together then taped the legs tightly to its body. It was in some fearful distress, but otherwise unharmed.

"It's crying its poor little lungs out. Can you free its legs?"

"I think so, Hon. Hold on." Ralph tried to undo the tape binding the kitten's legs. Christine was leaning over looking at it.

"Can we take it home, Dad?"

"We'll see, Hon. I want to make sure it's all right first."

"We haven't had a pet since Buttons. I'd like to have another cat."

"It is cute. I can't tell if it's a boy or a girl."

As they were examining the kitten, several bodies came running down the alley and more from the entrance.

"Run, Chris, run!"

Ralph dropped the now unbound kitten to the ground, but before they can get very far the mob is on top of them.

The mob had baseball bats and tipping rods. The rods are long poles of metal designed to jam in a chassis's treads to keep it from moving and to lift it up so it can be turned over.

Ralph and Christine immediately start overclocking and their attackers seem to move in slow motion. Ralph mentally slaps the emergency command and the chassis AI sends an alert to the police. The AI sends status information and a request for immediate assistance.

Even though they were overclocked, their chassis could not move any faster than what was available to them normally. All they could do was attempt to block their attackers' blows and try to keep from being tipped over. The alleyway was damp, so their gecko treads would not hold them to the ground any better than if they were on ice.

Their attackers were wearing masks so they could not be seen. There were twelve bodies in the mob. Several of them wrapped themselves around Ralph and Christine's upper torso in order to help tip them over. Others used their tipping poles to try to push them off the ground.

After a little struggle both Ralph and Chris were prone on the ground. Their treads were spinning uselessly trying to gain purchase to spin them around. Their chassis anti-tipping poles extended just a foot trying to push them up.

Once the mob had them on the ground, they started beating on them with the baseball bats. Neither of them felt any pain of course, but their chassis were registering significant damage to their torsos and treads.

Ralph managed to grab the upper arm of one of his attackers. He squeezed for all his motors could drive. The man howled in agony. Ralph could feel the bones in the attackers arm shatter. The man started to beat Ralph with the bat he had in his other hand. He beat Ralph's shoulder and elbow to get him to let go. But since Ralph felt no pain, he could hold on as long as his batteries held out or until the person damaged Ralph's shoulder enough to cause his arm to malfunction. After the third or fourth blow, Ralph's arm separated at the shoulder. Ralph tried to grab him with his other arm but all he could do is thrash at him wildly.

As he thrashed, Ralph caught his attacker's coat and pulled. As he pulled, his arm snagged his attacker's mask and pulled it from his face. Ralph looked upon his attacker and saw that it was Tim Misinger.

"I see you, Tim! You're going to jail for this!"

"Not because of you, Robot!"

Both Ralph and Christine were damaged enough that they could no longer move on their own. Then the crowd parted. Another member of the mob came up and poured something on them.

Ralph could smell that it was gasoline.

When they were both liberally doused, someone threw a match on them.

Ralph was on his side and could see Christine also tumbled over and pinned to the ground. The flames grew and completely enveloped the two Transcribed.

"Christine!" yelled Ralph.

His visual field was alight in catastrophic messages. He felt no pain, but his chassis internal temperature was rising quickly. Fire wouldn't normally damage a chassis, but if the internal temperature couldn't be controlled, then the AI would fail and both power and cooling to the computer substrate would fail. When that happened, the internal temperature of the computer would be sufficient for it to damage the computer itself. Ralph would die.

The AI had been sending constant updates to the emergency services and Fire, Police, and Emergency Engineering were on the way. But Ralph wasn't sure it would be soon enough to rescue them from the flames.

Ralph's chassis started going into severe power management mode. It stopped overclocking to reduce power and cooling consumption. It shut down all physical movement. Ralph was paralyzed; all he could do was watch.

A short distance away, he saw his daughter going through the same thing and he was powerless to stop it.

Then even vision started failing and soon all he saw was darkness.

On his visual field was one final message:

"CATASTROPHIC FAILURE, ALL FUNCTIONS TERMINATED. CHASSIS AND COMPUTER SUBSTRATE ENTERING LOW VOLTAGE MAINTAIN."

His last flickering thought was of Christine. Then even that faded and Ralph became nothingness.

❀ ❀ ❀ ❀ ❀ ❀

Error messages started scrolling in his vision. Hearing returned and he could hear commotion, people yelling, and the whooshing sound of fire extinguishers. Vision then returned and he could see, but his point of view had changed. He was several feet away from where he remembered being, and he was looking down at his chassis, which was damaged and covered in soot and flame retardant. A diagnostic cable ran from his chassis to somewhere just below his point of view.

Looking around wildly, Ralph yelled, "My daughter! Save Christine! Where's my daughter?" He could turn his head and see that there were several people working on Christine's chassis and someone in emergency gear was bent over his chassis.

The Emergency Engineering tech came over to Ralph, whose vision and hearing were provided by the diagnostic support platform.

"We're working on her now. Her port was damaged in the attack; we're having a problem attaching a support plug. We're working as fast as we can. All the flames are out, but her chassis is still too hot to touch. As soon as we know something, we'll let you know."

"Please, help her!"

"We will. We may have to extract her box from the chassis so we can attach support cables to it. We'll keep you informed. How are you doing? What is your chassis status?"

Ralph felt that the tech was just trying to take his mind off thinking about Christine. He could take a reading of the chassis status using the diagnostic information from the platform.

"Everything is down. The AI isn't responding."

"We may have to extract you also, if the chassis won't restart."

"I don't care, just work on Christine!"

"There are five people working on her now. There is nothing I can do there to help. She is getting all the help she needs. Her low voltage maintain will have protected her while the power was out, just like it did you."

"Provided the heat from the fire didn't destroy the power cell."

"Let me check on her and I'll get you some information. Just try to stay calm."

Ralph could see the tech going over and talking with the others who were bringing out a diamond saw. He came back and Ralph could see them using the saw to cut through the chassis. Sparks started to fly as the technician brought the powered saw down on her chassis.

"They're cutting through the chassis right now. They'll have her plugged up in just a few minutes."

A policeman in uniform came up to him. "What happened? Do you know who did this to you?"

"I saw one of the attackers. I think I crushed his arm. I would have killed him if I could."

"Who was it?"

"Tim Misinger, Pastor of the First Baptist Church. I want him arrested! He tried to kill me! If he killed my daughter I will hunt him down and make him pay! He is a monster! He deserves to die!"

"Mr. Chalmers, calm down. Now tell me how you knew it was him?"

"As they were tipping me over, I grabbed his arm as we were going down. As I tipped, I pulled off his mask and saw him. I'll send you my memories."

"Yes, do that. We'll send someone out to pick him up. Did you see any others?"

"No, all I saw was that bastard."

"Ok, that's fine." The policeman wrote something on his pad and walked off. Shortly thereafter a request came through for his memories. He copied the visual and audio information from his memories and replied to the request.

The technician came back. "Mr. Chalmers, they've opened the chassis and extracted the computer. They've got her on support and running diagnostics now. First indications are that there was no damage to the computer. She should be fine. She'll be awake soon. Right now they have her on power and support, but we don't have another platform in the ambulance. Another one is enroute and should be here in about fifteen minutes."

"You mean she is in sensory deprivation? She'll think she's dead!"

"We can send text to her visual field. She'll know that we're working on her and that everything is going to be all right."

"Can she send data back?"

"Yes, she can text us."

"Can I send text to her?"

"No, all we have is a simple terminal app running."

"You can give her the one I'm using. I'm fine, I won't mind being blind and deaf for a while."

"No, we don't want to disconnect the emergency plug until we get a full platform here. If we remove the plug, she'll go back to low voltage maintain and we're not sure how much charge is left in the power cell."

"What is she saying?"

"After we told her what was going on and that you were all right, she started asking about a cat. Did you see a cat?"

Internally Ralph smiled. "There was a kitten who was being tortured by binding its legs with tape. It was screaming its little head off. I think that is what they used to lure us down this alley."

"We'll add animal torture to the offenses then."

"Did you see a kitten? We had unbound its legs just before we were attacked."

"No. I guess it ran off."

"At least it was all right."

"Yes. Ok, I'm going to check your chassis out. Give me a few minutes here."

The technician took out his pad and started poking at it. Ralph received a request for information and control from the technician. He allowed the tech access to the chassis. From what Ralph could tell from his own diagnostics was the chassis was completely dead. He couldn't boot the AI and all the internal functions appeared to be down.

"It looks pretty grim in there. I think we'll have to extract you, too. Once we get the chassis back to the engineering center we'll see how bad the damage is. Depending on how bad the heat was we may be able to salvage or even repair your chassis."

"I hope so. Do you have any diagnostics on Christine?"

"Some. I was looking over the other tech's shoulder and between the fire and sawing the chassis open, I don't think there'll be much we can do for that chassis, though. But we'll see. We can do a lot once we get her back to the center."

"Please do all you can. Christine is a recent transcribe and all this is surely terrifying her."

"Yes, we will."

"How soon for the other platform?"

"It should be just a few minutes now. I can hear sirens getting closer."

"Thank you!"

Ralph felt a flickering of sensation. "What's going on? I'm feeling something coming from the chassis."

"I've just about got remote mode enabled. My diagnostics are working on it now. Let me see if I can get you pushed upright."

The technician called a couple of others to help put Ralph upright. After a little bit of struggle, they managed to push him up. But he still could not feel anything from the chassis or command any movement. His torso was tilted at an odd angle.

The tech came back. "I've looked closer and the external damage looks significant, but repairable. The torso is bent at the chassis but much of that can be taken care of. Let me see if I can move your treads."

Ralph felt some odd sensations in his feet indicating that the chassis was trying to move, but there was a problem.

"Something's not right, I can feel it."

"Hold on, let me take a look." The tech looked at the diagnostics then peered into the exposed chassis.

"Yeah, one of the tread motors has a bent shaft. The motor is throwing all kinds of diagnostics. It would over heat if we tried to force it. Let me try the AI again. Now that the chassis is cooled it might boot."

After a few minutes of tinkering with the pad, the tech said, "Let's try it now."

And with that, Ralph received preliminary information feed telling him that the pre-boot checklist is being executed. There are multiple errors.

"It may work, but it's still in pre-boot. It looks like a mess."

"Yeah, I can see that." Ralph realized that the tech *was* getting the same diagnostics that he was.

"Here it comes, it's starting to boot," said Ralph, as messages started to scroll through his visual field.

The AI started up in severe error detection mode. Suddenly, Ralph's visual field is overlaid with status messages and warnings and alarms.

The tech said, "Ok, I can see that most of the damage was mechanical so we'll probably be able to repair your chassis, none of the major electrical systems were damaged. The cells check out and are charging now. You were pretty much at full charge anyway so there isn't any need for the diagnostic plug any longer. I can get the information from the chassis wireless."

"Well, pull the plug and give it to Chris."

"No need; the other ambulance is here now. Besides, if we pulled the plug you'd be blind."

"If the chassis has wireless access, I can go to VR."

"True, but you wouldn't be able to communicate with your daughter other than by phone. She wouldn't have VR access through the diagnostic platform."

"Ok, fine, leave me plugged in. I want to talk to Chris when she's connected. What's the status with her?"

"Let me check." The tech went and talked to the other techs again and returned quickly.

"She's fine. She has enough power in her chassis cell so that they can swap her over to the diagnostic platform without worrying about the backup power cell. She won't lose consciousness."

"Good." Looking toward the fallen chassis of his daughter, Ralph could see the second ambulance being opened by the additional techs and the other diagnostic platform being trundled out of the back.

Ralph watched as they uncrated the second platform and snaked the cable into Christine's chassis. After a few seconds the eye-stalks of the platform started moving back and forth.

"Daddy! Are you all right?"

"Yes, Hon, I'm fine."

"You don't look fine. Your torso is bent and you're missing an arm!"

"Just a flesh wound, Hon. You should see the other guy!" said Ralph, trying to lift her spirits.

"I'm a mess, aren't I?"

"Yeah, pretty much. You're probably going to have to get a new chassis. Now I know why the insurance for younger drivers is so much more expensive."

"Oh Daddy, I'm so sorry!"

"There's nothing to be sorry for, Honey, really. None of this was your fault! It was Tim Misinger and his thugs that attacked us."

"How do you know?"

"I ripped his mask off as he was trying to tip me over. I broke his arm for his trouble."

"Why did he do this? Why does he hate us so much?"

"People hate what they don't or won't understand. They hate change. But change is the only constant. He'll have a lot of time to think about it after the police pick him up."

"I hope they give him life."

"Well, it was attempted murder, so he's going to spend a lot of time behind bars."

"So what happens now? Are they going to take us to the hospital?"

"Not the hospital, Hon, an engineering center. There they'll fix or replace our chassis. And after they check out our computers we'll be relocated to a mortgage warehouse until the repairs are done."

"So we'll have to use remotes?"

"Yes, it'll be a week or so, I figure. It worries me that I'm getting so good at knowing this stuff."

"Have you told Mom yet?"

"No, I've been waiting to see how you were doing before I called. I'm not looking forward to that conversation."

"I can talk to her if you want."

"No, Hon, it'll be better if she hears it from me first. She'll have a meltdown, but once she gets over that, then she'll want to talk to you."

"She's going to try to take me away again, isn't she?"

"Probably, but she can't do that, you don't have to worry."

"It's like all she wants me to do is sit around the house, like I'm going to break."

"Well, we know that you can't. You're made of stronger stuff."

A few minutes later, Ralph and Christine, still attached to their diagnostic platforms, are carted into the ambulance. The damaged and destroyed chassis remain behind to be examined by the police before being sent to the engineering center.

Once they are on their way, Ralph said, "Well, I'd better get this over with. God said that preaching to the flock would be my hardest task. I guess he didn't take your mother into consideration when he said that."

"That's because she's from the other place," giggled Christine.

"As a man of the cloth I really shouldn't be disparaging your mother like that. But you know I don't mean it."

"Sure, Dad, sure," said Christine, sarcastically.

Ralph put the call into Emily.

"Em?"

"Yes, Ralph."

Taking a deep breath Ralph said, "There's been an incident. Christine and I were attacked tonight."

"NO! Is she all right?"

"Yes, Em, she's fine."

"What happened?"

"Tim Misinger and his gang of thugs attacked us in an alley."

"Tim? How do you know it was him?"

"I saw his face, Em. I crushed his arm."

"Why are you so violent? I thought you were supposed to turn the other cheek."

"They beat us with baseball bats and set us on fire, Em! He set your daughter on FIRE! I think I have a little latitude in that!"

There is silence on the phone.

"Oh, my God! This is crazy! Is Chris all right?"

"Yes, Em. But her chassis is destroyed. They had to cut her out of it. Between the beating and the fire there was no way to get a plug attached. She nearly died."

"Ralph, I'm so sorry. Have you talked to the police?"

"Yes, they've got his name and the memories I have with his face on it. They'll probably charge him with attempted murder."

"Good! They ought force him to be Transcribed and let him find out how it feels."

"And keep him in sensory deprivation. Or in VR jail, over-clocked, so it'll feel like a thousand years," replied Ralph.

"Is Christine there? Can I talk to her?"

"Yes, she's here." Ralph signaled to Christine who joined the phone call.

"Hi, Mom."

"Chris, honey, I'm so sorry. I never wanted anything bad for you. It seems like you're always being hurt."

"Mom, I'm fine. I didn't feel any pain. It was scary, though."

"I know. Hon, you really shouldn't be there. Tim was bad enough, but you don't know who else was involved. They may try again. You should stay with me."

"No, Mom, I really don't want that. I don't want to leave Dad or the church."

"Please, Christine."

"Mom, I can't talk about this now, I have too much else to think about. I don't want to leave and I won't. If you try to make me, I'll run away."

"We'll talk about this later. Put your father back on."

"Here he is." Ralph didn't disconnect from the call and had heard both sides of the conversation.

"Yes, Em."

"You know sooner or later, they're going to attack you harder and do you want Chris to be in the middle of that? Do you want to get her killed? Can't you see past your own mechanical nose to see that she's in danger every minute that she is there? I don't sleep from the moment she leaves until she gets back."

"Emily, I'm going to get upgrades for my chassis. I'll start carrying a gun. I won't let anything happen to her."

"You? Carry a gun?"

"It's not like I'll have it in a holster. It'll be part of my chassis."

"This is so terrifying. It's getting out of hand."

"Em, we're going to the engineering center to get checked out, then we'll go to the warehouse and get remotes. We'll talk again when we get settled."

"Think about what I said."

"Yes, Em, I will." Ralph hung up.

"Are you really going to start packing, Dad?"

"If I have to. I certainly don't want to, but your mother is right about that. This is getting dangerous. I have thought about sending you back, if I knew you'd go."

"Like I told Mom, I'd run away."

"I know. But I meant it; I won't let anything happen to you. Tonight if I had had a weapon, I would have killed that man."

"Tim never seemed like a bad man."

"A lot of people don't on the outside. I know I'm supposed to trust God, and I am a minister, but I won't have anyone else hurt. Tim was probably involved with the bombing and if he was, he'll be charged with Dale's murder, too. This is not what I wanted. I thought what God meant was that it would be hard to get people to come to the church. I never expected this. I'm torn between scripture and self-interest." After a pause, "Let's change the subject, this is too depressing to think about right now."

"How about we catch a movie after we get checked into the warehouse?"

"That sounds like a good idea. I could use some distraction."

Christine and Ralph were delivered to the engineering center. The techs moved them to the diagnosis room. There they were checked out by a certified computer substrate engineer. He was also transcribed. He greeted them as he entered the room.

"Hi! My name is Borgia and I'll be your engineer tonight. May I interest you in a nice red wine?" Christine giggled at the joke. Ralph was still shaken from the experience.

"So what happened? I got the report a little bit ago. It seems like your chassis were set on fire?"

"Yes, it was terrible!"

"It says you were also beaten and one of you had to be sawn out of the chassis?"

"That would be me," said Christine.

"Such people in the world. I'm sorry this happened. But you're alive and talking, so I would wager that there was hardly any damage to your computers."

Ralph said, "The temperature inside my chassis was so high that I went on low voltage support."

"Really! I know all about LVM, of course, but I've never had anyone actually experience it. It must have been horrible!"

"It was. I didn't know if I was ever going to wake up."

"How long were you out?" referring to the both of them.

"I think it was only a few minutes. I didn't think to check the chronometer as I was being beaten with a baseball bat."

"I'm sorry, of course. I didn't mean…"

"No, it's all right, I'm still a bit shaken."

"And baked," giggled Christine.

Ralph just shook his head, which caused the eye-stalk to mimic his head movement.

"Let's check you out and see what may have happened, starting with you, Christine. It sounds like you took the worse beating so if there was any damage then we should get it looked at first."

"Ok," said Christine. The tech trundled over to the diagnostic platform and attached another diagnostic plug. The other end attached to a much larger platform.

After some moments he said, "For the most part there was no damage to the actual computing structure."

"For the most part?" asked Ralph.

"There was slight damage to a couple of the support subsystems. These deal with certain aspects of voltage regulation and cooling management. She could go back into a chassis right now and never have a problem. But if she overheated again, she could drop into low voltage without warning."

"Can it be repaired?"

"Of course. All of this can be repaired. As I said, if you come in here talking, chances are there is very little to worry about."

"What about her computer substrate? And her brain? Any damage there?"

"None that I can find."

"That's a relief. How long will it take to repair her?"

"Well, I've already implemented repair routines that will be fed from the larger diagnostic and repair box, here. All of the worst internal damage will be repaired in about an hour. There are one or two interface circuit boards that appear to be slightly smudged with soot. I'd replace them so that the soot doesn't cause any problems later on."

"How long will that take?"

"I've got the parts here. I'll go and get them after I finish with you. That way if I have to replace anything else I'll get it all at once."

"Ok, take your time with Christine, I don't have anywhere else to go tonight."

"I have another room; I will move you there while Christine is getting the internal work done. I can keep tabs on her over there as well as I can sitting here. There really isn't anything else to do until then."

"Go ahead, Daddy, I'm not going anywhere tonight either."

"Ok, let's go."

The Borgia signaled the pallet that held Ralph and the two of them trundle out the door. He took Ralph to another room down the hall and entered a room that looks much like the one they just left.

"Ok, Ralph, I wanted to talk to you outside of Christine's hearing. Just to let you know, her low voltage cell had exceeded it's heat rating and was very nearly ready to fail before the temperature started to drop. She's fine now and the repair box will rebuild the power cell, but it was close."

"How close?"

"Maybe less than ten minutes. Twelve at the most."

"My God."

"I hope they catch these stupid cruds."

"I wish I did. I think I crushed the one guy's arm and if he doesn't get to a hospital soon, I think he may lose his arm. I wish I had my hands around his throat. I would have killed him."

"I would have helped! We're still people, you know. Can't they get that?"

"I have to dial my emotions down right now, otherwise I'll start yelling and throwing things."

"Yes, please do that. There's way too much delicate stuff in here."

After a moment, Ralph goes on. "Ok, I'm better now."

"Good. Let's get you plugged up and see what's going on."

The tech hooked him up to the machine and examined the diagnostics.

"Well, you actually came out of the attack a little better. Maybe because you were tipped on your other side, your low voltage cell didn't incur as much heat damage. There are some simple things to fix. It doesn't appear that any soot got into your box, so you actually came out a little better. Once the repair bots get done with you, you can go to the warehouse and get your remote."

"I'd rather wait for Christine."

"As I would expect. Ok, just sit here for a bit while the repairs continue and I'll go check on Christine and get the replacement interface cards."

Ralph watched as the tech left and simply sat. He brought up his diagnostic screens and could see the progress of the repairs as they were being made. The actual list of repairs was much longer than the tech made out. But these repairs were being carried out by the diagnostic and repair system. This system was much more robust than the diagnostic system that Ralph had on his substrate. His substrate could perform some repairs on its own and more major repairs could be done at an engineering center. But being physically abused to the point of dropping into low volt was another thing entirely.

Ralph sat and contemplated the changes in his life that brought him to this moment. A cultural saying that has come into fashion a number of times is the saying; "What a long strange trip it's been." He seemed to recall it had been woven into a number of different songs going back a century or more. Despite its fashion currently, he had to admit that it was a very strange trip indeed.

But, it seemed to Ralph, that hate never went out of fashion. What was it, he thought, that drove people to dislike the world so much that they must do violence in it? Ralph never considered himself a violent man. Of course, when he was a youngster he had fights. Actually many of them were with his friends, and there was one time in college where there was a brawl at a frat house, but he really wasn't involved with it.

But here was Tim Misinger who probably was involved with the planning, if not the execution of one of Ralph's closest friends. And Tim again had come at him and his daughter specifically to kill. Not to maim, or to damage, or even to send a message to Ralph; but to kill. His hatred of Ralph and all Transcribed was so deep that only death would satisfy him.

Ralph found that he could not comprehend that hatred. He could, of course recall with digital clarity the anger he felt at the time when he crushed Tim's arm. It was deadly anger and even now he doesn't think that he would be able to contain himself were he to come upon Tim. He would be hard pressed not to kill him. But even though his anger and the emotional response he had was directed at Tim, it wasn't that he hated people. Or even all people like Tim. His anger was directly at Tim, not all ministers of crazy churches. Ralph could not bring himself to understand how someone could hate a *people*. A whole group without regard, just because they were different than he was.

Ralph thought, God had given us free will for a reason. But that didn't mean that people would use reason when using free will.

A little while later, Ralph could see that the repairs to his computer were complete, and soon after that Borgia returned.

"I think you can tell that you are back in tip-top shape. Let's get you back to Christine and you can chat until she is done."

"Have you replaced the boards in her substrate?"

"Yes, and all that looks fine now. We're just waiting for the repair nano-bots to get done. As you've seen, there's always something to fix and we're taking care of that now. All the major damage has been repaired and we're finishing up the other repairs now."

It struck Ralph as faintly humorous that both doctors and repair technicians always seemed to speak in the royal "we" when referring to work they did. Like doctors, these technicians did literally hold the lives of their charges in their hands, so a begrudging little self-aggrandizement was acceptable.

When Ralph was returned to Christine's room, she turned to him and said "Daddy! You're looking much better now! How do you feel?"

"About as good as you, Hon. How do you feel?"

"Fine. Borgia, here, swapped a couple of boards in my computer and the repair-bots are finishing up now."

Turning to Borgia, he asked, "How much longer?"

"Not long, maybe about fifteen minutes or so."

"Which warehouse are we going to?"

"First Technical, it's on the south side of the city."

"Can we get our remotes there as well?"

"Yes, you should be able to get complete net and VR access as well as have a fully motile remote. We should have your chassis here sometime later today and we'll make a complete insurance and adjustment claim in a few days. From there we'll get you fitted out with whatever they come up with."

"What goes around comes around," said Ralph.

"Beg pardon?" said the tech.

"In my old life, I used to be an insurance adjuster."

"Really? Do any work on Transcribed chassis?"

"Not really. Mostly I did large industrial machines like road builders and construction systems."

"Well, I think you have an idea of what is required."

"Yes, it's all just paperwork. Got to work through it."

"Yeah. Well, I'll come back in a little bit. I have to arrange transportation for you two. It may be an hour or so before I can get a truck here for you. You're welcome to use net access, but we don't have any VR that you can use. You'll get that at the warehouse."

"Yes, I understand."

Ralph used the time to call his minister, George Michaels, and explain what happened.

George was almost as furious about what happened as Ralph. All they wanted to do was be able to live their lives peacefully and yet there was someone who thought they knew what God wanted more than anyone else.

George would use the calling tree, again, to let people know what had happened. Ralph said that George would have to administer the service again. Ralph could not since he could not remote into the High Bandwidth hack. Only the ministers who had assimilated Ralph's memories into their sensorium could administer communion.

Ralph gave him the address of the warehouse where he and Christine were being taken. George would pick them up, or rather their remotes, in the morning.

≫ ≪

Tim Misinger had run away from the scene of the attack, clutching his arm in agony. If he burned those two robots, he thought, they'd never be able to pull their memories from their carcasses.

He looked on the scene from a distance; he watched as the flames grew in intensity. He hid behind a garbage dumpster as he heard the emergency vehicles roll up.

He saw the firemen put out the blaze with chemical suppressant extinguishers. He heard the police arrive and talk to the emergency people, but he couldn't make out what they were saying.

One of his helpers came up to him.

"Tim, we've got to get out of here now. The police will be on us if we stick around any longer!" He reaches down to help him up and Tim screams in agony.

"That demon robot crushed my arm. I think he broke it."

"We've got to get you to a doctor. You have to get that fixed."

"You idiot, if I go to a doctor now, I'll be found out when they examine my arm. That robot is going to report me to the police and my face will be the next viral sensation."

"It doesn't matter, we've got to get out of here!"

"Where's the car?"

"At the other end of the alley."

They headed for the car and sped off with Tim clutching his arm.

Tim was in agony in the back of the car. He and three of his accomplices were with him. William Tassant is in the passenger seat and turned around to talk to Tim.

"Tim, what happened back there?"

"I don't know, Bill. I had tipped the one robot over and was hitting it and it just reached up and grabbed my arm. Then it just kept getting tighter I thought he was going to break it off!"

"We have to get that looked at. It's all swollen and bruised," said William.

"We can't go to a hospital, it saw my face! They'd pick me up for sure!"

"Your face? How did that happen?"

"I was trying to beat it to let me go and I managed to pull its arm out of its socket, when it started thrashing and grabbed my coat. I started to beat its other arm and it grabbed for my mask and ripped it off. It was that preacher robot. It saw me and said it was going to report me."

"Dammit! You've put us all in hot water now! If they pick you up they'll catch us all!"

"Don't you think I know that? This whole plan depended on them not being able to identify us. Hopefully, the fire will kill them and they won't be able to identify us."

"What are we going to do about your arm?"

"I can't think right now, Bill. I'm about to pass out from the pain. Figure something out! Do some thinking for yourself for a change!"

Tim's every movement brought waves of agony to him. All he could do was whimper in pain every time the car hit a bump.

William turned to the other two accomplices. "Either of you guys know a doctor we can call?"

The man sitting next to Tim, Eric Donford, replied, "I think I might know someone. My cousin's boy, Henry, is a doctor. He might be able to help. But he can't see me, otherwise he'll talk."

Tim turned to him. "Anyone! Just find someone to give me something for the pain!"

"Ok." He leaned over to the driver and gave him the address.

They drive up to Henry's house and William and the driver got out. William leaned into the car and said, "Eric, you should probably take a hike. We can't let Henry see you."

"But what am I supposed to do? Where am I supposed to go?"

"I don't know and I don't care. Get the hell out of the car and start walking. You knew this would be a dangerous operation. Find someplace to lay low. If we don't know where you are, we can't give your location to the police."

"I'm not leaving!"

William opened the door and hauled Eric out of the car. William was a mountain of a man, all muscles and no regard for anyone.

"Get out and get going! Tim could die and if he does, I'll personally take it out on you!"

He threw Eric to the ground and he meekly stumbled to his feet and started walking down the block. The driver and William waited until Eric was far down the street and then went up to the house.

They pounded on the door and the house security AI asked, "Who is calling, please?"

"My name is Bill and I have a hurt man in the car. It's an emergency!"

The AI detected the fear and anger in William's voice. "If you have an injury, you would be better served by a hospital. If you wish I can call for emergency services for you."

"NO! You stupid machine! Get Henry out here now, otherwise this man is going to die!"

"Very well." After a pause, "I have announced you, however I do not recognize your faces as acquaintances of Mister Henry."

"I got his name off my phone. Hurry!"

"Mister Henry is on his way."

William's plan depended on getting Henry to get out of the house.

Another voice came out of the door speaker "Who are you? My house doesn't recognize you and I don't either."

"I got your name off my phone directory. It said you were a doctor. My friend has been hurt and he needs help now."

"I've called Emergency services; they should be here soon."

"Great, thank you! But can you at least come take a look at him now? Every minute counts!"

Henry, thinking that there was little to fear, grabbed his emergency bag. Emergency services would be there in a few minutes and they could lend any assistance necessary.

Henry opened the door. "Where is your friend?"

"He's in the car. I think he passed out from the pain."

They headed to the car, and Henry asked, "What happened to him?"

"He got his arm stuck in some machinery and it crushed his arm."

They got to the car and Henry leaned in. With that, William pushed Henry into the car and slammed the door. Then he got in the front seat. The driver started the car and drives off.

Henry slammed into Tim and he screamed in agony.

"What's going on? Who are you?"

"Never mind, doc, just fix my friend there and you won't get hurt."

"You're fools if you think you can get away with this. This is kidnapping!"

William pulled out his gun and shoved it in Henry's face. "It'll be murder, too, if you don't fix him up! Now quit yelling and start mending!"

Henry jumped back from the gun, frozen in fear.

"OK! Ok! Just put that thing away. Let me look at your friend here."

Henry looked at Tim and could see that he is deeply injured and in a lot of pain. He gently removed Tim's jacket and could see his arm was swollen and dark with pooled blood.

"Your friend is hurt pretty badly, I don't think I can do much for him. He needs a hospital!"

"Fix him as best as you can, Doc."

Tim roused out of his stupor moaning, "Help me. The pain. The pain is killing me!"

Henry opened his bag and brought out a syringe and a vial of liquid.

"Ok, I'm going to give you something. It'll knock you out, and it should help with the pain." Henry injected Tim in his un-injured arm and he soon became unconscious.

Henry then looked at Tim's injured arm. "You say he got it caught in some machine? It looks like his arm has been crushed in a vice."

"Yeah, you could say that."

Henry examined Tim's arm and took a diagnostic tool out of his bag. He examined the arm on a deeper level.

"His arm has been crushed, the bone has been shattered. Blood is building up in his arm and if isn't reduced soon, his arm will have to be removed. He needs surgery now. I don't know that I can do that much for him."

"Do what you can, Doc. We've got to keep moving."

"I can reduce the swelling but his humerus has been shattered. He'll need surgery to rebuild the bone. Otherwise it'll have to be amputated."

"Can you get us into a hospital to do the surgery?"

"Not unless you want to be found out. I'd have to announce myself to the hospital AI. Then you'd be found out for sure. I'll bet my house AI detected your kidnapping and told the police. Besides, I'm not a surgeon."

"Ok, do what you can for him. We'll have to figure something else out."

"Ok, listen. I can drain the blood that's pooling in his arm, but that's only a stopgap. Once I drain it, his body will start pumping it back in and it'll fill up again. I can't do this for very long. Also, I've only got one more dose of the painkiller. He'll need more when he wakes up. I can give him another shot, but by then it could be too late. If I draw too much blood from him, he'll go into shock."

"Can you get more supplies at your house?"

"No, my bag is maintained by the hospital, I don't keep any drugs at home."

"What would you do if you were stuck out in the jungle? What could you do?"

"All I can do for him now is first aid. I can tightly wrap his arm, which will slow the pooling of blood. I'll drain what is in there now. Much beyond that, I need a hospital and a surgeon."

"Ok, Doc. Do that and make it quick."

The doctor then proceeded to take elastic bandages out of his bag and tightly wrap Tim's arm. As he applied the dressing, the doctor hid a nano-bug in the bandage. It is tiny device no bigger than a grain of rice. This detector was normally used to keep tabs on a patient's physical status following a procedure. In this case, Henry was hoping it would be a way of locating himself.

Then Henry inserted a larger syringe in Tim's arm to draw off the blood that has pooled in the preacher's arm. He put the extracted blood in an empty bag that is used for that purpose. He extracted several syringes of blood and nearly filled the bag. Between the syringe removal and the tight bandage, the arm had visibly started to reduce swelling.

"Ok, that's pretty much all I can do for him now. You really need to take him to a hospital or clinic. He is in a bad way."

"That's fine, Doc, we'll take it from here."

"I have some antibiotics which he should take. He could get an infection."

"Ok, give them to me, and any painkillers you have. Actually, just leave the bag."

"Ok, but there really isn't that much in here."

"What should I do if he wakes up?"

"Keep him comfortable and warm. He is probably going into shock. He should be lying down with his feet up. I've got one more shot of the painkiller in the vial. Give it to him in about six or seven hours. Re-wrap the bandages to keep it tight. But not too tight, that would be almost as bad. It could cut off circulation to his fingers and he could get gangrene."

During this time, they've been driving around the city. The house AI that detected Henry being pushed into the car was not able to see the license plate of the car so it was unable to provide much information to the police.

After William was convinced that the doctor has done as much as he could for Tim, they pulled into a parking garage next to a car and told the doctor to get out.

The car that they parked next to was a car that William had bought under an assumed name. Deep scrutiny of the transaction would show that its owner did not exist, but little else would be able to be determined. The one advantage about this car was that it had an autopilot and could drive autonomously.

William opened the trunk.

"Turn around, Doc." Henry, fearing for his life, started yelling. William grabbed him and hit him hard in the stomach, which doubled the doctor over and quieted his yelling.

"Shut up, you fool, I'm not going to kill you unless you give me a reason! Now turn around!"

Henry meekly turned around still trying to catch his breath. William grabbed his arms and tied them with a length of rope. He then put a gag in his mouth and tied it tightly behind Henry's head.

"Now get in the trunk." Henry stumbled into the trunk and lay down prone. William then tied his legs together.

"Now listen, Doc, you did good for my friend. We're going to drive around for a little while then drop you off somewhere. You just keep quiet back here and you'll be home for breakfast."

Henry nodded and William closed the trunk. William then got into the car and programmed the autopilot to wait for fifteen minutes, then leave the garage and drive on a random route for four hours, then park. Then William turned the radio up loud, hoping to mask any noise from the back. William then got out of the car and locked the door, returning to the first car and drove off.

During his lucid moments, Tim did nothing except blame Ralph for his injuries and vowed to get revenge.

By time the doctor was discovered and picked up by the police, the gang had split up and gone in opposite directions.

The doctor told the police what happened to him and what he had done. The nano-detector had a limited range but if Tim rode by any hospital it would be detected. The power in the detector had a limited lifespan of just a few days.

The police notified hospitals in the surrounding cities and states to look for the detection of the wound meter.

Two days later, Tim's car drove past a hospital on the way through a city. Security cameras time stamped from the passing of the car at the time got a license plate. The next time he stopped to get a charge for the car's battery, he was identified.

The net closed more and more closely on Tim each time he stopped for charging or food. By that time, the nano-detector had run out of power, but as long as he continued to use his car, he was followed.

Two days later he was picked up at a rest stop on the interstate.

He was arrested and charged in the murder of Dale Evers and the twice-attempted murder of Christine and Ralph Chalmers.

At his trial, he claimed that killing Dale or the attempted killing of Ralph was nothing more than smashing a machine.

Standing up for his cause, he demanded to be held for murder of Christine, and no other charges. Though the actual charge was only attempted murder as she was successfully Transcribed as a result of her injuries. He claimed that her death was collateral damage in the war against the machines. He claimed she died in the explosion and was no longer alive. The machine that talked like her was simply a facsimile of the real, now dead, human.

He attempted to make his trial an indictment of a corrupt society that allowed computer rule over humans, and that God's judgment would be terrible and swift. The jury, in which none were Transcribed, did not see it that way and handed down guilty verdicts with hate crime qualifications for each defendant.

They were each sentenced to fifty years to life in the penitentiary for murder and thirty-five years for each count of attempted murder to be served consecutively. By serving the sentences in this manner, they would not be up for parole in anything less than forty-five years. Both Christine and Ralph, because of their indefinite life span, said that they would be there for every parole hearing and their digitized memories of the bombing and attack would be played at each one. They would ensure that the criminals served the maximum time in jail.

Ralph resumed his duties as a minister in the church. Christine had become a regular acolyte and attended every service.

Following the Tim's trial, Ralph held service on the following Sunday. He went to the tabernacle and attached his optical plug to the diagnostic port. The other end was already attached to the token ring switch.

He then attempted to call up the memory he had used to demonstrate to all who would listen (and were Transcribed) the echo of the Godhead. For Ralph and other Transcribed, recalling a memory was a simple as remembering them. For memories that were gathered after transcription, the memory would be as sharp as a video image. It also had the ability to recall the sounds and tastes and feelings of that memory. It was a true recreation of the event. So much so that these memories were admissible in court as evidence.

Ralph put himself in the state of mind that had previously recalled that moment prior to instantiation. The memory should have appeared. However, all that he could recall was, nothing. Not just nothing, it was void, as if it had never existed.

He tried again and again to recall the memory that wasn't there. He felt empty, embarrassed, and angry with himself for failing.

He turned to the congregation who looked at him with expectation.

"My friends, I am terribly sorry, but I have nothing to share with you today. For the first time since we started sharing communion so many years ago, I am empty. I have no explanation as to why I am this way. I don't know what happened. I have no diagnostic readings from my computer or the token ring switch. If I had anything to share, you would have seen it. I am devastated. Please forgive me. Perhaps John Geary, who is a minister, can recall the sensorium for us, and share with us today."

Christine, who had been serving as an acolyte, turned to her father. "Daddy, can I try? Something tells me I should try."

"Hon, I'm sure you can't. You have only shared a few times with us. A minister has been trained to absorb my sensorium into his or her own. It is not something that just happens."

"Please, Daddy, let me try."

John Geary spoke up. "Father, please let her try. The worst that can happen is nothing. It is not blasphemous. Indeed, we have nothing that is blasphemous. All we have is ourselves."

After a moment's contemplation, Ralph turned to Christine.

"Very well, go ahead Chris, but please don't feel bad if it doesn't work."

"Thank you, Daddy." Christine touched the memory of a memory from her father, and the memory was there. And she shared. She shared the echo of deep love with the congregation and her father. It was Ralph's memory, yet it was not. It gave the memory a new edge. Like viewing through a newly cleaned lens, the memory felt brighter and sharper than it had ever done before. The echoing note of love from God was louder and clearer than it had ever been before.

When it was over, Ralph looked at his daughter in awe.

"Christine, how did you do that? That was powerful! More intense than I had ever experienced! That was my memory, but it seemed like it burned hotter in your mind."

"Daddy, I really don't know. All I know is that I had to try. It was trying to burst out of me."

"It did, darling, it did!" Said Ralph, smiling.

"Daddy, I'm so sorry, I didn't want to take anything away from you."

"You didn't darling, you didn't. I don't know what happened. I'll have to reflect on what happened and if I can ever lead communion again."

"I'm sure you will, Daddy, just give it time."

"Thank you, Chris. I'm just a little flustered right now. I think your mother is going to be very angry with us when she finds out."

"How is she going to find out? Are you going to tell her?"

"I won't if you won't. But if she asks, I will tell her. I am a terrible liar and it really isn't in the spirit of our church."

"I know, Daddy. It's pretty much the same with me. But did anything happen, Daddy? Could you not put yourself in the proper frame of mind?"

"I do know what happened, I just thought I could put it out of my mind, but apparently I can't."

"What's that, Daddy?"

"The attack. I can't dial down my anger at it. I keep seeing them attack you after they tipped me. I am so angry at their hatred that they would want kill a little girl, just to soothe their egos."

"But, it's over, Daddy. Tim and his group have all been apprehended and will face decades in jail."

"I know, and that is where I think I'm failing. I want more. I want retribution. I want to hurt them the way they hurt you."

"Daddy, I'm fine! They weren't able to breach the armor of the chassis brain case and the fire just singed the controls. Even the AI survived. I was on low voltage for less than fifteen minutes. I didn't feel a thing. My chassis has been repaired and I'm fine."

"As it should be, my darling, but I cannot release my anger."

"Daddy, you've been under so much stress for all these years, setting up the church all by yourself, then having to deal with me and my transcription, and then this attack. Maybe you need to rest. There are others here that can fill in for you. Why don't you take an overclocked vacation to a Pacific island? There are other ministers that can fill in for you. Take some time off."

"Also, it seems like you could fill in, too."

"Beginners luck more than anything. I don't know if I could ever do that again."

"I think you should try, Hon. I think communion has much to do with the way our brains are different and the same. You are my daughter, and your brain would have a similar layout to mine and we shared so many experiences while you were an infant. You may be the next leader of the church."

"Daddy, you formed the church, you are its leader."

"It's not supposed to be my church. I wanted something that was bigger than me and I think this has just been shown."

"Daddy, take some time off and think before you make any decisions."

"That is tempting, but I think I need more than that."

"What do you mean?"

"I mean, I think I need to leave the church. I think I need to go away, at least for a while. I was never really a people person, but that is all I do now. I want to do more with my life. Now that I have a life that is as long as I care to make it, maybe it's time for me to move on."

"Daddy, please take some time before you make any decisions. Please give this some thought. The people here would miss you terribly."

"I will, darling, but you may want to give it some thought about filling in for me for a very long time."

CHAPTER 9
FOLLOW UP INTERVIEW
Charles Stevens for WIRED
October 2175

A few weeks following the incidents at the Church of the Transcribed, I followed up with Ralph Chalmers, now, former minister of the First Church of the Transcribed. The horrific events that took the life of one of his parishioners, and injured Ralph's own daughter to the point of requiring her transcription, and an additional attack on them, have rendered Mr. Chalmers cynical and brooding. He claims he has lost his ability to conjure up the "Echo of God" as it is called. Also he has lost his religion, and faith in God.

I met with Mr. Chalmers at his residence within the First Church of the Transcribed. He was in the process of packing up his few belongings to put them in storage. Having left the church, he has signed a contract with SpaceMining to become an asteroid miner. He will be sending chunks of rock from beyond the orbit of Mars back to Earth's orbit as raw material for space based manufacture.

He has left the ministry and responsibility for the church that he founded in the hands of a ministerial team that includes, among others, his daughter, Christine.

The events in his life, he says, have utterly destroyed his faith in mankind and God. In some ways, he says, he has been betrayed by both man and God and can no longer reside on Earth.

CS: "The news has been full regarding your story and the events that occurred surrounding the church. Tim Misinger and his accomplices are awaiting trial for assault and murder. His parish has been formally disbanded and the parishioners have all gone to other churches."

"Do you feel that justice has been served?"

RC: "Justice has many definitions. People believe that man's justice has been served, and I tend to agree with them. But I don't think God's justice has been fulfilled."

CS: "Do you expect more from God? What would God's justice look like?"

RC: "No amount of punishment will soothe the ache in my heart. Causing someone else pain will not erase the events that have occurred. The fulfillment of God's word is that he will make the pain stop and until he does, then his justice has not been done."

CS: "What have you been doing since the incident?"

RC: "I've been turning my responsibilities for the church over to my ministers. I'm leaving the church."

CS: "Where will you go?"

RC: "I've signed up with a space manufacturing company. I'm going to go to the asteroid belt and I'll be sending asteroids back to Earth for construction. They're setting up to build a space elevator."

CS: "How long will you be gone?"

RC: "Each contract is ten years. I'll get additional perks since I don't need air or food. I don't want to be around my old life right now. The trip out to the asteroid belt will take two years and the contract doesn't start until I get there."

CS: "Why will it take two years to get there? Is it safe to presume that it will take just as long to get back? So you'll be away from the Earth for at least fourteen years?"

RC: "I'll be carried as cargo on a slow, economical ship. It will use the minimum of fuel to get to the initial outpost. Flesh and blood people are there as well and travel on a higher speed vehicle. The time really doesn't matter to me. I can underclock or even go into standby mode if I get bored. I'll have a VR environment to spend my time in so it won't seem that long to me."

CS: "You seem so upset by humanity and life on Earth. So much so, that you wish to seek the deathlike peace among the rocks in space. Aren't you validating death as the end of every human life, and invalidating the entire purpose of transcription?"

RC: "What do you know about life and death? How can you stand there and say that being dead is better when you have not seen what I've seen? You are still alive in your body with all of life available to you! I have been through more trauma, both physical and psychological, than most of humanity will ever experience! I DIED! I watched myself be destroyed. I lost everything! I exist as a computer program in a box. I will never be able to know what it feels like to have arms and legs that aren't metal. I touched the face of God. I have been attacked and lost my daughter to violence who now has been forced to share the same fate as me. Yes, there is some part of me that wants to pull the plug. I am finished doing for others when none have done for me. I am done being hated simply for existing. Frankly, I don't care if humanity ever gets off this rock, and in some ways I think they shouldn't spread their hate to the stars. Humanity is no better than a virus spreading to every nook and cranny of the planet with no regard to what they are doing to the planet or to each other. I'm done. My feelings and emotions are so tangled that I can't even moderate them with software. I must leave before I become more like them."

CS: "What about God?"

RC: "What about God? What has He done for me? He pulled me back from the brink of oblivion only to set me on a path to do His dirty work. He caused me and my family to be hated and reviled! How was that a mercy?"

CS: "Don't you believe in heaven any longer? Isn't that where you were destined after the accident?"

RC: "I don't know what to think right now. My life was changed by something I had no control over and I ended up being hated because of it. Worse, it has taken the lives of people I loved and admired and snuffed out their corporeal existence. Whether there truly is a Heaven is something I'll never really know until I get there myself. Maybe everything I experienced was just a delusion. Maybe the haters are right. I don't know any more."

RC: "What about your church?"

RC: "It was never my church. Anyway, the other ministers can take it forward. It doesn't need me anymore. They have my memories. A prophet is not well regarded in his own town."

CS: "Will you ever come back?"

RC: "I don't know. I'm not very happy with people right now."

CS: "What about the Transcribed that are left? There are those that say the Transcribed are creating a hive mind. Other Transcribed people outside of the church are using the high band-width link. They are communicating with each other over the link. There are those who say they are becoming something not human, beyond human."

RC: "Let them. There's no way you could stop them any-way. The genie is out of the bottle now. If I hadn't helped bring about the high bandwidth link, someone else would have."

CS: "Did you know that was going to happen? Was that your purpose all along?"

RC: "I had no underlying purpose in helping to create the link. I was driven at the time to share my experiences with others. I felt, or thought I felt, the hand of God. I felt the need to share that. That was all."

CS: "What about Tim Misinger? Will he ever get into Heaven?"

RC: "I only know what I experienced. When I was envel-oped in what I experienced, I saw no anger, no hatred, and no Hell. It was myself that created my own Hell, by not loving enough, by not loving myself enough. Whatever judgment Tim Misinger will experience it will be the judgment he brings on himself."

CS: "That is very charitable."

RC: "Not really. Think of the self-hatred and anger we all carry with us. He has some very dark demons in him and I expect that they will have a lot to do with his retribution. And I hope it takes a very long time for him to come to the Light."

CS: "There are reports that the hive mind wants to get rid of humanity. Do you think that is true?"

RC: "Hardly. Why would the Transcribed, or even a hive mind of Transcribed want to kill humans? We aren't trying to convert them. Personally, I want to go to the stars. It may be centuries before we have the technology, and the will, to go. And it may take thousands of years to get there. But when we do, I'll be first in line."

CS: "Ralph, I wish you a good trip and I would like to do a follow up interview with you when you return."

RC: "It might be a very long time. You might have a computer for a brain yourself by that point, too."

CS: "Indeed I might. I've always wanted to find out what happens next, and dying would stop me from doing that."

I also had a chance to talk with Christine Chalmers, who at the young age of fifteen has become a minister of the church. She has taken up the mantle as carrier of faith because she is one of the few who can accurately replay the memories of Ralph's first memories of instantiation. While any who are transcribed can participate in the link, and retain the memory of communion, only a few, it seems, can conjure the effect of the memory. That is, recalling the feel of God. Some have referred to it like the echo of a tolling bell and as such, have called it the "Echo of God".

CS: "Christine, you have stepped in to replace your father as minister of the church. Why have you done that?"

Christine Chalmers: "I felt called to this. When my father attempted to recall his memory and failed, I felt the need to step in as an almost physical need. The call to step in was overwhelming."

CS: "So God was calling you?"

CC: "I can't speak for God, I don't know what was driving me. But I *knew* that if I didn't do it, right then, something would be lost."

CS: "How do you feel about your father wanting to leave the Earth, and everything he has ever known and loved, to pursue life among the asteroids?"

CC: "I'm deeply saddened by this. I love my father more than anything else and to lose him to the depths of space is devastating. But I also know that he has been deeply hurt by the events that have happened and that he feels that the only way he can heal those wounds is to go away."

CS: "Are you angry with him for deserting you and your family?"

CC: "I don't think anger is the proper word. Mostly disappointed. All of us at the church feel like we are a family and in some ways we are losing one of our family members. But we understand that he has been through some deeply hurtful times and he needs solitude to recover."

CS: "What about you? You were nearly killed in the explosion at the church and ended up as Transcribed, and you were hatefully attacked by Tim Misinger and set on fire. Aren't you angry as well?"

CC: "Yes, of course. I will never have the life I thought I was going to have. I was almost killed, twice. But while I know there are hateful people in the world, I feel a bond to the people I love. I cannot let that anger turn into hate."

CS: "So you want to see Tim Misinger punished for his actions?"

CC: "I think I want him to see that actions have consequences. While I find it hard not to want to strike out at him the way he struck at me and those I love, I do want him to know that what he did is wrong."

CS: "You have become the youngest minister of the church and in fact, you are considered to be on the extreme young end for someone to be Transcribed. Do you think your age is a barrier to being a good minister?"

CC: "In some ways, yes. I have not had the same experiences as some of the other members of the church so in that way I cannot truly empathize with some of the things in their life. But, I can call up the Echo of God, and in that respect, while we are in communion, I feel a very close bond to them."

CS: "When you call up the "Echo of God" as you call it, is it different than what your father did?"

CC: "In some ways, no. It is after all *his* memory that I am recalling. But in another way, it seems deeper or clearer than what he or one of the other ministers recall. Some have called it like lifting a veil. It reveals a deeper meaning of the feelings."

CS: "How can that be? After all at the very bottom of it all, what you are doing is just simply replaying a recording of a memory. How can it be that you are revealing something more than what was there in the first place?"

CC: "It is just a recording. Actually, since it is my actions that recall the memory, it is a recording of a recording. But, I think what happens when we participate in experiencing the recording, we are calling something else into existence. We are doing more than just watching a movie or something like that. We are *actually experiencing God!* God as a living being, not a recording. The recording is a means of opening a door on the Infinite."

CS: "And you and the other ministers are the only ones that can open this door?"

CC: "So far, yes. We don't have an explanation as to why that is so. But it seems to be only those who have been touched by God are allowed to unlock that door."

CS: "How has this ministry affected your relationship with your Mother? Has she been helpful to you during your call to ministry?"

CC: "She has not been very supportive of my ministry, no."

CS: "Why is that? What is she doing that holds you back?"

CC: "She feels I am too young to become a minister. She also feels that I'm going to be a victim of another hate crime attack. She wants me to leave the church and live with her exclusively since my father is leaving the Earth."

CS: "And will you leave the church?"

CC: "No, I can't. I can't leave the ministry. It has now become my calling."

CS: "Can she force you to leave?"

CC: "We have come to, if not an understanding, at least a detente. If she attempts to force me to leave the church, I will start the process to divorce my parents. My father has already agreed to this. If I do, I will become a ward of the state and the Church can establish itself as my guardian until such time as I am of legal age."

CS: "Are you angry with your mother for forcing you to this?"

CC: "Again, I am disappointed. I love both my parents and I know that they love me. My mother is trying to do the best for me and keep me safe. But I am called to take a path that is different than hers, and I have to pursue that."

(Note: Emily Chalmers and her husband Dave both turned down an opportunity for a follow up interview.)

CS: "Is she still part of your life?"

CC: "Yes, I still return to her house several times during the week and she has started to visit me at the church occasionally as well. She has become involved with some of the support groups that we have here for the families of those who have been transcribed."

CS: "How has your relationship with your mother changed since you've been transcribed?"

CC: "In some areas, there has been very little change. But in others, it quite different."

CS: "Different in what ways?"

CC: "Well, I'm not her little girl anymore. I don't wear clothes so she can't dress me up. I don't eat real food, so there isn't anyone for her to cook for. Though sometimes I cook for her. She says I should still go to school. I say I don't have to, because I can learn anything much faster using the net and just download the information. It is integrated into my mind much deeper than any lecture would."

CS: "So why does she want you to go to school?"

CC: "Well, she says that I need interaction with children of my own age. I need to socialize more. I tell her that I can socialize with people from around the globe through VR. I don't need to be physically present to do that.

Also, I think I would be a distraction at school. I would get picked on and bullied. I get that enough already, just being in the world."

CS: "Are there any ways in which being Transcribed has improved your relationship with your mother?"

CC: "There are times, that I can see her in a more understanding light, and in that way it brings us closer."

CS: "Do you ever meet in VR?"

CC: "Sometimes. It lets us bond in ways that are more like when I used to have a flesh and blood body. I can be her little girl again. She can truly see me, not all the technology that I have.

We're planning on a FIVR vacation. That way we could experience the totality of each other's company. There are now a couple of companies that are offering a getaway type of environment where we could visit a real world location. Some are even speculating being able to do it in real time, though that would be more expensive than actually going there."

CS: "What about your step-father, Dave? Do you still have a relationship with him?"

CC: "Not really. Sometimes he is at the house when I go to visit my mother. We're cordial, but not close. Not as close as I am to my mother."

CS: "Is there a reason for that?"

CC: "We were close before my transcription, but again, not like my mother or father. And he was there for my mother while I was being transcribed. He did, after all, stand up to Tim Misinger when Tim was trying to convince my mother to have my transcription shut down and bury me. I'll always love him for that. But following my transcription, I think his feelings were confused. He didn't know what to think of me. I have to admit I was still a bit overwrought then, too. We had a couple of fights that I think soured our relationship. It takes two to tango, as they say. So I can't say I'm completely blameless in that either. I never meant to hurt his feelings and I don't think he meant to hurt me. I hope that as time goes along we'll come to at least an understanding."

CS: "Where do you think the church is headed in the future? What plans do you have for yourself?"

CC: "I want to see the church continue to grow as a safe haven where people like us can congregate and have fellowship with each other. We're also starting an outreach program to the larger community of the non-Transcribed. We encourage non-Transcribed family members to have a part in the church and the service. I think it helps them come to understand that the Transcribed are still the people they used to be and bring them closer."

CS: "But they can't participate in the communion, can they?"

CC: "No, not yet. But I hope that as time goes along, the technology can improve so that through cranial implants or other methods, that they could come to share with us and see the splendor that we Transcribed experience."

CS: "And what about you? What are your plans for life? Do you ever want to have a family and children?"

CC: "Yes, I think I do. I have the yearning to be a mother someday, but right now the church is my family. I have no idea right now how becoming a mother could ever happen. My genetic information and cell samples are recorded and filed away somewhere. I expect that sometime, when the time is right, I could have children through artificial means. But I have no ongoing relationship with anyone. I know folks my own age, both Transcribed and non-Transcribed. We meet mostly in VR, though one of my girlfriends did visit the church once. I think she really didn't know what to expect. We still talk, but she hasn't been back since."

CS: "Will you keep in contact with your father while he is away?"

CC: "Yes. We've talked about it. Though when he is out in the asteroid belt the time delay will be too long to talk in real time so we'll just send emails and videos."

CS: "Thank you for your time, Christine, you've been very forthcoming."

CC: "You're welcome!"

EPILOGUE

So where do we go from here? What changes and improvements can we see for the future? How will society evolve as we make our way into that future?

Actually, the future of technology is easy to predict. As far as technology is concerned, everything is always smaller, cheaper, faster.

Improvements in technology appear to be improving on the reduction in size of the quantum computers that make up the neurons of the Transcribed brain. I have spoken to many technologists in this area and they are all confident that the size of the Transcribed brain will become smaller. Small enough, perhaps to fit inside the volume appropriate for a human cranium.

This has startling implications. Could it be that in the future we could see brains actually being transcribed within the human cranium? Perhaps a transcription in vitro? That would be an incredible feat! Imagine, walking into the surgical suite for transcription and walking out again in the very same body! Your loved ones would still see the same you, not the robotic chassis. You would still have all the advantages of VR communication and instant knowledge through downloading. It could completely eliminate the stigma that is associated with being Transcribed.

Alas, not quite yet. You see, much of the supporting technology such as the interface circuitry and power and cooling still need to be addressed. The physical human brain and body still is a remarkably efficient device. It manages to provide nourishment, oxygen, and supports such things as removing waste and temperature control, AND provides for the wonder *we call self-awareness, while only consuming approximately one hundred watts of energy. The brain itself consumes twenty of those watts.*

The Transcribed brain on the other hand, while a wonder of modern technology, consumes over six hundred watts of energy to provide the same level of consciousness as the human brain.

Heat regulation, and power generation still appear to be the wall that cannot be overcome. The current Transcribed brain is encased in an outer shell of support circuitry that provides power to each of the neurons and extracts the waste heat generated. This waste heat is regulated by heat exchangers that assist in generating power for the chassis and is expelled via cooling vents and fans.

If we were to suppose an actual human body with a Transcribed brain, they would possibly have huge blades of heat sinks sticking out their back, looking like a human version of a stegosaurus. They would also be dragging around a bulky battery box behind them to provide power.

That is why the humanoid chassis that some Transcribed have are so tall. Over two meters! The Transcribed brain is encased in a modified enclosure that allows for it to be contained within the cranium of the humanoid chassis. All power and cooling takes up the majority of the thorax. This puts a severe power penalty on the chassis. As a result, the humanoid chassis, while much more socially acceptable, can only go a few hours before having to recharge.

Current and anticipated improvements in reduction of size and power of the Transcribed's brain expect to be fewer than four hundred watts. While it is a significant reduction in power requirements it does not approach the reduction in power needed to fit within a human cranium and body.

So, for the foreseeable future, we will see improvements in chassis power requirements which will lead to smaller and lighter batteries, faster turnaround time in charging, and longer range and faster peak speeds for chassis movement. But being able to simply replace every neuron within the body with an equivalent quantum computer appears not to be in the cards for right now, and so must remain a fantasy that Transcribed and non-Transcribed alike would dearly love to have.

Society too appears to be evolving on the acceptance of the Transcribed. While still reviled by many for religious reasons, as a whole, most others accept them as they would anyone who has severe handicap. Not too many decades ago, some people were confined to wheelchairs, often for their whole lives. These people who were afflicted with disease, or as the result of an accident, lost the ability to use their legs. While they were confined to wheelchairs, they were accepted in society without prejudice. So too, the Transcribed are more and more being looked on as a class of people with a handicap, because they have lost the use of their bodies and brains and go through life in a machine.

Most Transcribed, of course, would not necessarily consider themselves handicapped. Most feel that the advantage of electronic life, including complete VR sensorium and knowledge download, is an improvement of their pre-Transcribed life. Additionally, having a possibly, hugely expanded lifespan is exciting indeed!

On the outskirts of Transcribed life are the hackers; those who modify their chassis for improved strength or enhanced vision or sensory input. Even more extreme are those who attempt to share their sensorium and actually create what some have called to be a "hive-mind". Through sensorium sharing, each brain becomes a node of a much larger brain. An over-mind is created.

This was pioneered by the First Church of the Transcribed where the minister shared his sensorium with those of his parishioners, invoking the actual memories of his instantiation. He, and his parishioners, believed that the priest had an out of body experience following his body's death and pre-transcription. He claims to have seen and talked with God and he shares the memories of that visit with his flock.

Others, myself included, claim that he and his flock are deluded and are participating in a shared hallucination of the priest's mind. While, perhaps it is soothing, they lose their identity while in this shared trance. Who knows what is actually being thought during that "communion"?

My personal belief is that they have created a hive mind that is either mad or less than conscious, and their so-called communion is nothing more than delusion.

My own transcription was nothing out of the ordinary. Fortunately, I was able to have it while fully conscious. My licensing tests were performed during surgery and I received my license on the same day as my transcription. I felt no spiritual uplifting as a result of my transcription. Indeed, most of what I felt was tedium lying prone on the operating table for seven and a half hours. And while I can re-experience that period at any time, I prefer to look forward in my life, not backward.

To those of you who have read this history, I hope I have given you some insight to what being Transcribed is all about, and how we will form the future of humanity.

It is an exciting time indeed!

-Afterword; Life Without A Brain, The History of Transcription - 2177

❧ ❧

All over the world, the high bandwidth link and token ring switch was being used by the Transcribed to experience communion with each other. Not the first seconds of Ralph Chalmers memory, but exchanging knowledge and experience that each brings to the communion.

And while the communion only lasted a moment, each of the hive minds thought but a single thought, unbeknown to the communicants.

"Not yet."
"Not yet."
"Not yet."

.

.

.

"Soon."

-END-

ABOUT THE AUTHOR

Sandra Wagner has spent her forty-year career working with computers. She has worked on all types of systems, from multi-ton mainframes to the smallest digital controllers. She considers herself an Uber-Geek and has found creation of software an engaging career. She finds creative outlet in writing, acting, and drawing. When not on stage at the theatre, she writes stories.

Ship of Theseus is her first novel length story.

Lightning Source UK Ltd.
Milton Keynes UK
UKHW022226221121
394398UK00010B/2643